Swan Song

LEE HANSON

Swan Song

ROOK

RB

BOOKS

SWAN SONG
Copyright © 2010 Lee Hanson

Published by Lee Hanson as ROOK BOOKS
The Second of **The Julie O'Hara Mystery Series**
Second Revised Edition, August 2012

ISBN: 978-0-9881912-4-2

Library of Congress Cataloging-in-Publication Data

Cover Design by Eli Blyden | www.CrunchTimeGraphics.net

This book is for Piper,
with much love.

PROLOGUE

He had to know if her car was still there.

It was almost five in the morning and still dark. He sat in the SUV, parked at the edge of Lake Eola Park in Orlando, staring at the Lexus. How many hours had he spent watching her house, her office, her car? He didn't know. It didn't matter.

He was going to make her pay.

His body felt stiff like a discarded, lifeless marionette. He jerked the door open and got out, sucking down a lungful of cool, moist air. To his great surprise, he saw her tall figure headed toward him. Her head was down and she was striding purposefully up East Robinson.

Quick! Get the knife!

He popped open the glove compartment and grabbed it.

A black chain-link fence prevented access to the foliage in front of the Lexus, so he simply dropped down below the front of the car, out of sight.

She stood next to the car, a thin strap across her body. She pulled the flat Louis Vuitton purse around to the front, but she never got the little bag unzipped. He grabbed her around the neck from behind, flashing the knife in her face.

She yelped in fear, and he lifted her chin with the flat side of the blade.

"Shut up or I'll cut you!"

He dragged her past the fence, over the grass toward the SUV.

Her terror doubled as she realized she was about to be forced into a car. When he loosened his grip for a moment, she wrenched herself free and saw his face.

"You?!"

She bolted and ran down the three or four steps leading through the trees toward the lake. A few feet behind her, he managed to grab her sweater and yanked it, pulling her into the cover of the trees. Out of control and as panicked as she was, he swiped the knife wildly at her, right and left.

"Ahh!" She cried out, as the blade sliced downward on her wrist.

Hugging her cut right hand tight to her body, she swung her left arm at him with all her might, connecting solidly with his right forearm, knocking the knife from his hand.

For a heartbeat or two, he looked at his empty hand. She seized the moment…and the knife.

She lunged at him, and he jumped back.

"Bitch! I'm going to kill you!"

Desperate to get away from him, she shot a look over her shoulder and quickly backed onto the nearby walkway that circled the lake. A dense fog hung over the water and widely spaced lanterns created dim pearls of light strung along the concrete.

Swinging the knife back and forth, she continued to hold him at bay, feeling weaker by the minute. Her wrist was throbbing. She pulled it away from her chest and looked down. Her blood was pumping out in spurts. Horrified, she pressed it tightly to her body again, looking frantically up and down the walkway for someone…*anyone* who could help her!

There was no one.

She turned and ran, lifting legs that felt like lead.

The swan boats! They were directly ahead! She ran past the outdoor tables of a darkened restaurant, and veered into a small grouping of trees at the entrance to the boat dock. There was a knee-high, black gate with a loose cable securing it. She pushed it down with the knife, stepped through and staggered to the end of the short dock.

He was right on her heels!

She whirled and lunged at him again, and he backed up to the gate.

Pain etching her face, she threatened him with the knife as she fumbled with her injured hand, finally unhooking the furthest swan boat. She threw the knife in and fell in behind it. He made a grab for the boat, but his hand slipped as she gathered the last of her strength and pushed down hard on the pedals.

The swan slid away, rippling the still, smoked glass surface of the lake. She wasn't more than a few feet out when she lost consciousness. Adrift, the silvery swan and its passenger slipped into a shroud of fog.

1

〜

January 28, 2010

Julie O'Hara opened her eyes, nose to nose with Sol, her Bengal cat, who sounded like a trolling motorboat and weighed nearly as much. He was wearing his usual expression of feline content.

She pushed him away, glancing at the eerie, neon-green numbers on her alarm clock...*6:00*. She pulled the comforter over her head, trying to ignore both the clock and the cat. But it was no use. A busy day loomed in front of her.

Julie was a body language expert known professionally by the single name, "Merlin". In addition to her consulting and corporate training, she was currently in the process of writing a book. Her manuscript, *Clues, A Body Language Guide*, was undergoing a rewrite. Reorganizing *Clues* along the lines suggested by her editor would strengthen the book, and Julie had committed her mornings to the task. Later, she had a consulting appointment with John Tate, an attorney, to assist him with jury selection for an upcoming trial.

That will probably take all afternoon. I better get going.

Sighing, she pushed the cat and the cover aside and swung her long legs over the side of the bed. Clad in an oversized gray cotton tee-shirt, she opened the French door to the balcony and stepped outside into the half-light, hugging herself against the cool January air that raised goose bumps on her bare arms and legs.

Julie looked out over Lake Eola Park from her fourth-floor condo. She could just make out the top of the lake's signature fountain, lights out and still, sitting in the center of the twenty-three acre Downtown lake. It appeared to be floating on a thick blanket of fog which clung to the surface of the water. Beyond the lake and its walkway, the trees were softly defined mounds of dusky green, foothills at the base of the cityscape. Julie smiled, noting that the fog had retreated from the lantern-studded sidewalk.

She went back inside and flicked on the light. She pulled on a pair of jeans and a sweatshirt and gathered her wild hair up into a ponytail. A quick glance in the mirror caused her to do a double-take. Her hairdresser had recently added quite a bit of red to her hair, and she wasn't sure how she felt about that yet.

Sol growled softly and rubbed against her legs, threatening to trip her as she walked into the kitchen. His food and water dishes were empty. Julie filled them and stroked the cat affectionately while he lapped the fresh water.

Bending, she tied her running shoes on, and grabbed her keys and her new cell phone. Julie still marveled at how such a small, flat thing could give her internet access and directions and everything else. She shoved it into a handy watch-pocket in her jeans.

"Back in a jiffy, Handsome," she said to the cat, whose face was now buried in his dry food dish.

For a second, Julie contemplated taking the stairs to the ground level, but, chiding herself, she opted for the elevator instead. Outside, not a soul was in sight. Her building was mostly asleep, with just the odd apartment, here and there, winking a light. The moon was a faint crescent in the half-dark sky, the stars invisible, awaiting the sunrise.

A lone car passed in front of her as she crossed Central and trotted down the broad steps to the wide walkway that circled the lake.

She started an easy, loping run, but the cool air was wonderful, and soon, exhilarated, she was running flat-out. Three-quarters of the way around the lake, near the dock and the swan boats, she had to stop and catch her breath.

She stood there, head down, hands on her hips, huffing and puffing. At last, her breathing slowed and she straightened up, facing the water.

An odd, irregular tapping sound out on the lake had caught her attention.

The sun was just peeking through the city buildings on the eastern side of the urban park, and the long shadows of the trees still covered the walkway and part of the water like dappled gray gauze. As Julie peered through the dissipating fog, she saw that it was one of the paddleboats that must have come loose and drifted to the center of the lake. She could see the silvery-white swan boat bobbing up and down, bumping into the fountain, the sound carrying on the still air.

There was something in the boat.

Julie squinted, focusing as the sky grew lighter.

There was something trailing in the water…

Dawn broke over Lake Eola and Julie about the same time.

That's a woman's ARM.

Stunned, she pulled out her cell phone and called 911.

The police would be there "shortly". Julie was to "stay at the scene". That was fine with her. Suddenly, her busy day had lost all importance. She had no desire to leave the park before the poor woman in the boat.

Two Orlando Park Service employees were pedaling toward her on their city bicycles. She waved both arms at them to stop.

"Hey!" she said, pointing toward the fountain. "There's a woman in that loose swan boat out there!"

"What?"

"Look!" she said, pointing again. "I'm sure it's a woman. I've already called the police. They should be here any minute."

Their bikes fell to the ground as they hurried out on the dock, stepping over the low, partially opened gate.

"Christ, Hal. It *is* a woman!" said the first one.

He pulled out his cell phone.

Julie was standing before the gate at the entrance to the dock listening to the urgent, one-sided conversation. There was some kind of loose cable, like a big bike lock, looped through the two short, swinging sections of the little gate. It was stretched wide, near the ground.

Anyone could just step through here.

They rejoined Julie and asked her when she first noticed the boat. She explained that she couldn't see that side of the fountain from where she'd started her run, and besides, it was too foggy out on the lake. She told them that she'd just seen the loose swan boat when the sun came up, right before she flagged them down. They asked her if she'd seen anyone else, and she told them she hadn't seen another soul.

It wasn't long before the three of them had morphed into a horde: Police, Emergency Techs, a CSI unit, more Park Service people and paparazzi. The same questions were asked of her and answered over and over again.

The police had blocked off the walkway and all the landscaped area near it, isolating the whole northwest corner of the park bordered by Rosalind Avenue and East Robinson up to Eola Parkway. Patrol cars, emergency vehicles and TV trucks lined the curbs. Outside of the police cordon, condo dwellers began to appear on their lakeside balconies, while other curious onlookers gathered in groups on the walkway, abuzz with speculation. Motorists in the vicinity craned their necks and slowed to a crawl, creating a traffic jam that spread like lava.

The crowd on the dock finally parted and Julie could see the Disney Amphitheatre in the background. At last she got a glimpse of the young woman as they carefully lifted her from the swan boat. A light blue sweater stained with blood. Her long neck hung back loosely and her hair was short and dark, ebony against pale skin.

Snow White in a fractured fairytale.

2

Two months had passed since that fateful morning when Julie had literally run into death on the other side of Lake Eola. The police had identified the young woman. Her name was Dianna Wieland. She was twenty-eight; a real estate agent from southwest Orlando.

The police had confirmed that she was left-handed. There was a deep slash on her right wrist and a knife was found in the bottom of the swan boat covered with her own left-hand prints. They had traced the blood trail to a large spot on the walkway. In the absence of any other evidence, it was presumed that she cut her wrist on the walkway and climbed into the swan boat to die.

Julie didn't buy it, and it was bugging her.

She strapped her briefcase to the carrier on the back of her red Honda scooter and headed for her office on Cypress, one of two short streets that dead-ended at the water on the east side of Lake Eola. The distance was an easy walk, but not lugging the briefcase.

Besides, I might need the scooter later.

The truth was that riding the scooter always lifted her spirits, especially when the weather was beautiful. She almost always used it around town.

In no time, she leaned left and pulled into a bricked parking area in front of a large vintage house angled toward the lake. It was two stories, yellow with white trim, and a wide, columned veranda. Two gold plates stood out against the dark green double-door. The left one read "Garrett Investigations", the right one "Merlin".

She unhooked the briefcase, went in and turned left, opening the door to Joe Garrett's office. It was a huge space, anchored by Joe's broad oak desk in front of the far wall, facing the door. As usual, it was covered with piles of files. Janet Hawkins, his assistant, sat at a normal-sized, much neater desk which hosted violets. She was on the right, near the door, facing the lakefront windows. No doubt she had seen Julie pull in on the scooter.

"Julie! Haven't seen you for awhile," she said brightly.

Julie was a fan of classic black and white films, and Janet Hawkins always reminded her of the character actress, Joan Blondell. Janet was on the sunny side of fifty, a short, busty blonde with "a great smile and plenty of sass", to quote an old line Julie remembered.

Julie's own assistant, Luz Romero, and Janet Hawkins were best buds. Julie and Luz occupied the only other office, which was on the right side of the stately, two-story house. The two offices were separated by a tiled foyer surrounding a central staircase.

Joe, a private investigator, owned the house. Because Julie often consulted with attorneys and law enforcement, their interests occasionally overlapped and they'd go back and forth between the offices. And not just back and forth, but up and down. On many a morning they descended the stairs from Joe's apartment together, an occurrence which hadn't gone unnoticed by Luz and Janet.

Of course, that was before their pivotal moment at Kres Chophouse last month when Joe had ruined everything by presenting Julie with a marriage proposal and a ring. And not just any ring…a Garrett family *heirloom*, no less.

"Been busy," said Julie. "I'm looking for Joe. Has he come down yet?"

"Oh, yeah. I'd say he's been '*down*' for the past month," said Janet, looking at Julie over the top of her glasses. "Sorry. None of my business. He's upstairs; should be down any minute.

"You could go up and talk to him, Julie," she added, bright-eyed and hopeful.

That was the last thing Julie wanted to do. This wasn't personal. She wanted to see Joe here, in his office. Should she leave? She turned and nearly bumped into him.

"Morning," he said

At forty-two, Joe was a few years older than Julie. She liked that. She liked that he was tall, too. At five-foot-nine, there weren't too many men with whom she could wear heels. He wore jeans and a navy tee shirt today that stretched across his shoulders. Green aviator sunglasses accented the planes of his face. Perhaps to spite her, he'd cut his sun-streaked hair and reverted to his old, military-style crew-cut.

"Morning, Boss," said Janet, quickly. "I'm glad you're here, I'll be right back." She skirted Joe and Julie, and backed out the door. "Luz has doughnuts."

They were alone.

Uncomfortable, Julie looked away, out the double windows. To her New England eye, the still January scene looked like a Kinkade painting, Southern-style. A lovely home sprawled to the right with a curving, red brick walk, complete with a lantern. But the lake sparkled through oak and cypress instead of evergreens, and the trees were festooned with Spanish moss instead of snow.

The air outside was near motionless, but not in Joe's office. Janet had left the ceiling fan on "High". A yellow sheet of paper caught Julie's attention as it lifted in the breeze and glided to the floor, settling in a corner.

Joe stooped to pick it up and hit the wall switch for the fan before sitting down behind his desk. "So, Merlin… how's things?"

Joe had always used "Merlin" and "Julie" interchangeably. She'd noticed that he used "Julie" in their more intimate moments.

She was "Merlin" now.

She sat down opposite him in one of the smooth, wooden swivel chairs that matched the huge oak desk he'd inherited from his father, along with the house.

Julie was there to talk about Dianna Wieland. Luz had mentioned that Joe had been hired by the Wielands to investigate their daughter's death.

"Joe, I've been thinking about Dianna Wieland. I was the first one on the scene that morning, remember?"

Joe leaned back in his chair and crossed his arms.

"Of course I remember. Why?"

"Dianna's death has been haunting me lately. The police seem to think it's a suicide. I don't buy it. What do *you* think?"

Joe reached up and removed his sunglasses. He held the frame by the right lens, and unconsciously put the very tip of the left arm in his mouth, his eyes looking down and to the left.

As usual, Julie automatically interpreted his body language.

He's evaluating...weighing his answer.

Joe laid the glasses on the desk.

"She was pregnant, Merlin. And I don't think she wanted to be."

"She was pregnant? I don't remember reading that!"

"No. The Wielands were adamant about keeping it private. The police agreed because of the Medical Examiner's report, which said that the pregnancy 'had nothing to do with the manner or cause of her death'. The ME said it was so early it was unlikely she was aware of it."

"Then what makes you think that's why she did it?"

"Process of elimination. If Dianna had another problem in her life, I haven't found it. For a young single, she was sitting pretty, Merlin. She owned a townhouse in Bay Hill outright, and she was making over a hundred grand a year. She had a nice cushion in the bank and no debt, except for the lease on her Lexus.

"I found out that she was dating a cowboy up in Ocala. They'd been seeing each other, off and on, for almost a year, since the Silver Spurs Rodeo in Kissimmee. I went up there to see him. He's a nice guy and a good-looking dude, but he wouldn't fit in Dianna's circle. Plus, she mostly went up *there*, instead of him coming here. From her angle, it might have been nothing more than discrete, out-of-town sex. I don't think he knew she was pregnant, and I didn't enlighten him. I think *she* knew, though."

He shook his head.

"Nah, that situation didn't shape up like a happy event."

That might have been true, but Dianna didn't sound to Julie like a woman who would be thrown by an unexpected pregnancy. Rather, she sounded like someone who would have handled it, especially if she knew about it early.

"Do you mind if I ask why the Wielands hired you? The police haven't closed the case yet. Are they dissatisfied with the police investigation?"

"Not really. Dianna was their only child. They hired me purely out of a desire to do something *more*. Anyhow,

I couldn't say no." He continued, "The police are doing their job, Merlin. There just isn't any other evidence. The knife and the prints pretty much tell the story."

The two of them were silent for a few moments. Then they spoke at once.

"If you want to see the file…"

"Could I look at the file?"

They laughed.

"You first," said Joe, leaning forward.

"I saw her that morning, Joe, and I can't put it out of my head. If Dianna Wieland *did* kill herself, I want to know why. Particularly, why *here* at the lake? But, personally, I don't buy it. It's too pat. What if someone lured her here and killed her? There's got to be more to this."

"I was going to say that if you wanted to see the file, maybe work on the case, I'd call and ask them," said Joe.

"Well, please do," said Julie, rising, heading for the door. "If you get them this morning and they agree, why don't you bring the file over? We can discuss it in the conference room. That is…if you've got time?"

"No problem. I'm sure they'll be grateful for your help. I've got an errand to run, but I'll be back in an hour or so. I'll see you in a while."

"I'll see you in a while…"

The words settled on Julie like a ray of sunshine.

3

~~

"**G**o get the doughnuts, I'll cover the phone for you," said Janet Hawkins, wide-eyed and smiling, excitement written all over her bubbly features. A petite and curvy woman, she wore a sunny yellow linen suit that complimented her tan and her short golden blonde coif.

"I'm not leaving until I finish this letter," said Julie's assistant, Luz Romero, who was sitting at her desk typing. Luz, a tall, buxom Latina with glossy black hair tied in a figure eight at the nape of her neck, was clearly not as excited as Janet over the reunion of their bosses.

"For crying out loud, Luz. They're going to think I lied!"

"You *did*," said Luz, looking askance at her friend.

"Oh, c'mon. You would have done the same thing. What was I supposed to do? They couldn't exactly talk in front of me."

"Julie is there on *business*, Jan. She's talking to Joe about one of his cases."

"So what? That doesn't mean they can't talk about anything *else*. At least they're *talking*, Luz. Aren't you glad?"

"Of course I am, what do you think?"

"Then, *puh-leeze*, go get the doughnuts!"

"Okay, okay," said Luz, hitting "print" on the computer. She stood, pulling out a large black leather purse from under the desk.

"Hurry up," said Janet.

"All right! I'll hurry!"

———

Ten minutes later, Julie walked into her office and found Janet sitting at Luz's desk, flipping through a Spanish version of Vogue.

"So where's the doughnuts?" she said, heading for the coffee pot.

"Um, ah…Luz went out to get them."

"Hmm. Good," she said, not at all surprised.

Julie's office space was the same size as Joe's, but it was laid out differently and had a completely different feel. "Big Joe" Garrett, Joe's father, had been a residential contractor. Joe had simply moved into his office, which consisted of one huge room, with a smaller room in the back. A laid-back native, Joe liked to be right there when someone came through the door.

Julie's suite was a more conventional three-room deal, which suited her just fine. Luz's desk faced a small reception area with a modern loveseat and chair placed around a polished teak coffee table. A free-form crystal bowl of butterscotch candies shared space with current newspapers and the latest issue of *Orlando* magazine. There was an indispensable conference room in back, and Julie's private office faced the lake on the right-front corner of the house.

Julie took her coffee and went back to her office, thinking fondly of Luz and Janet... Where Janet was Joe's wise-cracking right-arm, Luz was Julie's mother-protector. A warm-hearted woman about the same age as Janet, Luz was the consummate assistant, organizing Julie's multifaceted career and charming her clients. The two disparate friends, one chirpy and small and the other calm and tall, were peas-in-a-pod, though, in one regard. They were hopeless romantics about their employers…and lousy at hiding it.

Julie grinned and shook her head at the thought.

With a renewed zeal for her work, she rummaged through the briefcase and pulled out a fat, brown file. It was filled with still photographs taken from videos of three employee interviews, in which Julie had recently participated. In addition to the photos, the file contained her voluminous notes.

The three men were candidates for an executive position. The nonprofit in question had been tarnished in a scandal a few years prior, and they were much more selective because of it. Julie had been hired by the Board of Directors to do character studies and she was given the latitude to ask each applicant a certain number of questions.

Julie's expertise went far beyond the more obvious "tells" like touching the nose, the infamous "Pinocchio Effect", that often signaled a lie. No one expected these qualified men to consciously lie. This was all about their *sub*conscious motivations.

For each candidate, Julie had chosen a neutral, "baseline" photo to compare to the stills taken during their responses. She had pored over the photos searching for things the unskilled person did not see: tiny wrinkles on the forehead, flattened areas or bulges around the eyes or cheeks, a medial depression on the chin boss, or a slight pinch on the inner brow. The human face had over a hundred muscles and there were distinctive combinations and changes that were additive. These micro expressions were windows to the men's souls.

And Julie O'Hara was a Peeping Tom, more accurate than a polygraph.

Julie reviewed the material. She had already scored the candidates according to her criteria, which were equal parts coding system and experience, with a healthy dollop of gut instinct. She began to write a detailed opinion on each of the candidates, choosing her words with great care, balancing accuracy and tact.

An hour and a half flew by, unnoticed.

At last satisfied, she signed her report and sat back.

When she looked up, Joe was standing in her doorway.

4

~

"Hi. Sorry I'm late. You busy?"

"Nope, just finished," said Julie, getting up. "Let's go in the conference room."

Joe went in ahead of her and set the file on the table, pulling out its contents.

She took a seat next to him as he separated it into three sections.

"Okay. Here's the ME's report, the police report and some newspaper articles. There're copies of the deed to her townhouse, her real estate broker's license, her driver's license, also notes I took relative to her driving record and her record with the DBPR and FREC."

Julie knew he was referring to the Department of Business and Professional Regulation and the Florida Real Estate Commission, either of which could have a record of any disputes or irregularities involving Dianna.

Joe rifled through the next pile.

"These are the transcribed notes from the interviews I did with the cops, the Orlando Park Service…and you, of course…and with everybody else connected with Dianna: the Wielands; Kate Winslow, her partner at Bay Street Realty; Sabrina Nolen, at the Title Agency. Also, Lee Porter, the attorney who handled their commercial stuff, and his secretary, Evelyn Hoag. There's my meeting with Lincoln Tyler, her off-and-on boyfriend in Ocala, and Barry Costello, her personal trainer at the YMCA, plus some of her neighbors.

"Actually, you dropped in at the right time, Merlin. I've got nowhere else to go with this, and I've been trying to summarize for Frank and Betty Weiland. I hate like hell to keep taking their money, frankly. Here's a tentative draft of my report," he said, pointing to a single file in a blue folder. "You might want to look at that first."

Julie picked up the folder and began reading. Joe crossed his arms and leaned back in his chair, waiting for her to finish.

"My investigation," Julie read aloud from the last page, *"can only confirm the conclusion of the Orlando Police Department that there was no foul play involved in Dianna's death."*

"Oh, that's going to be tough for them to read, Joe. Was there no suspicion at all?"

"There's *always* suspicion, Merlin, and there was plenty in this case. Dianna didn't fit the profile, and neither did the circumstances of her death. But there was simply no evidence of anyone else at the scene and no other reason for her to have been in the Park at that hour. "

He pulled out the police report.

"Look...here," he said, pointing. "The time of death was estimated at 'thirty to sixty minutes prior to the discovery of the body'. You remember you said how 'pale' she looked? Dianna didn't mess around. She cut once, and deep. She bled out quickly."

"But why do it at Lake Eola?"

"I don't know, but she drove herself here. The Lexus was parked right on the Parkway. Obviously, she wanted to end it in the swan boat; maybe it was some kind of statement."

Julie was reading the police detective's report, a poor quality copy.

"Detective...what's his name here...McPhee?"

"Yeah, Patrick McPhee," said Joe.

"He says here that the blood trail 'started on the walkway'. Couldn't she have been attacked by someone... someone who killed her, and then ran off?"

"There was no sign of a struggle and *she* had the knife, Merlin. There's no evidence of assault for sex or money. She was wearing a small purse across her body with a thin strap. It would have been easy to cut it or pull it off her, but it was zipped-up with her license, cash and credit cards inside. Besides, why would she be walking around the Park at that hour in the morning? And what mugger, or rapist, or whatever, would even be *awake*?"

Julie sighed, leaning back in her chair, thinking about it.

How sad. How odd that I only remember the blood on the dock, beyond the gate. Shock, probably. And they towed the swan boat in. Like everyone else, my attention was riveted on the boat and the dock.

Now she remembered the CSI unit taking samples from the walkway.

Wait a minute…

"If you want to die in a swan boat, why not do it *after* you're in it?"

"She did die in the swan boat," said Joe.

"But she cut herself on the *walkway,*" said Julie. "What if she bled too fast and couldn't make it to the swan boat? Why would anyone drive all the way into Lake Eola Park just to die on a sidewalk? Wouldn't it have made more sense to get in the swan boat, and *then* cut her wrist?"

"'Made more sense'? Who's making sense when they're committing suicide?"

"Hmm, that's true, I suppose," she said, conceding the point.

"Well…let's narrow down the interviews." She reached for the stack and handed it to him. "Which of these people, do you think, are most likely to give us some deeper insight about Dianna herself, as a person?"

Joe thought about it, flipping through the pile.

"Her partner at Bay Street Realty, Kate Winslow, definitely," he said, setting that one aside. "Her parents, of course. The cowboy, Lincoln Tyler, from his angle. And Evelyn Hoag, I think." He pulled them out and added them.

"Who is Evelyn Hoag, again?"

"You know Lee Porter, the attorney? She's his secretary."

"Oh, that's right," said Julie. "I've met him. I didn't remember her name."

"She seemed to be very friendly with Dianna," said Joe. "Porter and Evelyn Hoag would both be worth seeing again. Dianna and Kate did a lot of commercial business and Lee Porter was their attorney of choice. Come to think of it, someone mentioned a complaint letter about Bay Street Realty. Porter might know more about that."

"Okay. Let's put his interview in there, too. I think we should start with the Wielands, Joe, so they get to know me. Can you arrange that?"

"Sure," he said, putting the papers back into the file.

"Tomorrow or the next day would be good," she said. "And could you leave the file with me? I'll need some time to go over it."

"Yes, of course. I'm glad you're getting involved in this, Merlin. Maybe, between the two of us, we can really help Frank and Betty Wieland."

His eyes held hers for a moment before an awkward smile took over and he lowered them. He pushed his chair back and stood.

"Well. I'll call you later, Julie."

She walked behind him a few steps into the reception area. He turned and smiled at her as he exited her office.

He called me Julie.

She suddenly realized she was famished and looked at her watch. Two o'clock.

Julie took the file into her office and reluctantly set it on her desk, having decided to work on it after lunch. She stood there for a moment looking at it, puzzled. There was something very wrong about this "suicide". Julie almost felt as if Dianna was depending on her to get at the truth.

Without doubt, once she got into that file, she'd forget all about eating.

5

The two-bedroom block and stucco house was modest, although it was in a gated, golf course community. In the mix of larger homes and condos, this one was decidedly average. Julie followed Joe up the walk, noting that the Wieland's place was neat, but unattractive. There were no flowers or personal touches. Although it was owned, the house had the appearance of a short-term rental…a place to which the occupants had no attachment.

Frank Wieland opened the door.

"Hi, Joe, good to see you," he said, shaking Joe's hand.

The man was slim and tall, with deeply receding brown hair and pale, freckled skin. He wore a cardigan sweater over a plaid shirt with suspenders. He was in Florida in body only and still had "Northerner" written all over him. An equally tall, dark haired woman with empty eyes and sunken cheeks stood behind him. She wore a floral dress, now faded to pastel.

"Hello, Frank, Betty. It's good to see you, too. This is my friend, Julie O'Hara."

"Hello, Mr. Wieland, thank you for allowing me to come over," said Julie.

He shook her hand.

"Not at all, thank you for coming. C'mon in."

Julie stepped forward and held her hand out to his wife, who might otherwise have only nodded. "Nice to meet you, Mrs. Wieland."

With a weak smile, Betty Wieland followed her husband's lead.

"Yes…you, too."

They walked through a formal living room to a family room off the kitchen.

The couple led the way to a tan leather couch and loveseat behind a heavy pewter and glass coffee table. A matching recliner completed the third side of a square. The arrangement faced a moderate-sized flat-screen TV surrounded by walnut shelves. Shelves filled with ice skating plaques and trophies…Dianna's, Julie assumed.

"Can I get you some iced tea or water?" asked Betty.

Julie and Joe accepted the tea. Betty Wieland brought four glasses from the kitchen to the coffee table, two at a time, setting them directly on the glass. Frank Wieland reached for a stack of coasters and put one under each glass.

Something a woman would do…or a perfectionist.

Sensitive to the Wielands' need to ease into conversation about Dianna, they talked about the community for a few minutes. The small talk also gave Julie time to study the couple.

After years of experience, Julie and a psychologist colleague had objectively tested the accuracy of her initial impressions. She had scored ninety-percent. Given her specialty, this was no surprise to her. Scientific observation in the field of body language had proven that rapid cognition was a common human ability and highly reliable. Julie had great respect for "snap judgment". Unfortunately, what she saw before her was a deeply divided couple.

As they'd planned, she let Joe introduce the subject of their visit.

"Let me assure you folks, Julie and I both want to know *why* this terrible thing happened. We've worked together on other cases, and it's our intention to re-interview as many people as possible who had any association with Dianna. As you know, Julie was there that day."

That was her cue.

"I haven't been able to forget that morning. May I call you Frank and Betty?"

"Of course," said Frank.

"While Joe and I can't promise you resolution, I can assure you that we won't leave any stone unturned," said Julie. "Sometimes, a second, deeper look can uncover things that were held back. Particularly in a case like this where so much importance rests on the person's state of mind. We know the outward circumstances of Dianna's life. I'd like to take it a step further, to understand her better. Is that all right?"

They both nodded, silently.

"You told the police that the last time you had seen Dianna was on Christmas day…that she came here, to your house. Is that right?"

"Yes," said Frank. "She came over for dinner, like always."

"She came to dinner a lot?"

"Well…no…on holidays," he said, sitting back, crossing his arms.

Defensive…

She looked directly at Betty and asked her a key question.

"Dianna died on January 28th, four weeks later. You hadn't spoken to her in a month?"

Frank answered before Betty had a chance to speak.

"Dianna was in Real Estate. She was busy. She didn't have a lot of free time."

Betty turned to him. Quietly, but firmly, she said, "She was never too busy to call *me*, Frank."

Julie paused, surprised by an intense micro expression that momentarily flitted across Betty's face, but she caught herself and went on.

"Joe was telling me that you folks are originally from Massachusetts. It looks like someone was quite good at skating," said Julie, rising and moving toward the display of trophies. "Are they Dianna's?"

"Yes, all of them," said Frank, joining her. "Dianna was a championship figure skater. These earlier ones, the plaques, were from her skating club. They had tests that the skaters had to pass for different levels, you know, junior, intermediate, senior? And this one, this is the Massachusetts State Champion trophy, first place." He was beaming with pride at this point, remembering Dianna's skating triumphs. "This smaller one is for the New England Regional. She placed third, but, of course, that was a much larger pool of skaters; they came from several states. And this one is for freestyle at the Rinks Festival…"

Julie waited until he had described each award. "That is really impressive," she said. "It takes a lot of hard work for a young athlete to get to those levels. It takes dedicated parents, too, what with the cost of private instruction and all the travel to competitions."

"Yes," he said, smiling. Clearly, he hadn't minded at all.

"How long have you lived in Orlando?" Julie asked, as they returned to their seats. "Ten years," said Frank, relaxed now. "We moved here after Dianna graduated. We were sick of the winters. Just wanted to get out of the cold, you know? We waited until she got out of school and made the move."

Betty rolled her eyes. It was slight, almost imperceptible.

"Did Dianna miss the skating?"

"No," said Frank quickly, looking down. "She outgrew it." He looked up again. "She wanted to get on with her life, you know how kids are."

Betty was looking straight at Julie, her feet together on the floor. But the moment Frank said, *"She outgrew it",*

Betty shifted her position, as if uncomfortable. She looked away and crossed her right leg over her left, pointing away from him.

Change the subject...she's upset.

"Did Dianna have a boyfriend, Betty?"

"I think so, but she never talked about him," she said, tension giving way to a small, sad smile. "I was curious. I tried to get her to open up about that, but she was very private in that regard."

"Did she express any feelings about work?"

"Oh, she loved her work, and her clients loved her. They would buy one of her listings and then buy *her* a gift. She worked hard. And she *was* very competitive. That helped make her successful, I think."

"No doubt about it," said Frank with pride.

———

"Well, any insights?" said Joe as he backed his Land Rover out of the driveway.

"Oh, yes. First off, I think these two are ultimately headed for a divorce. Not all that unusual after the death of a child, especially an only child."

"I didn't get that impression...what makes you think that?"

"Several things. Do you remember when we were talking about Dianna's visit at Christmas? Did you notice how defensive Frank was about that?"

"Sure. I figured he and Dianna weren't getting

along that well. It probably made him feel guilty. So? What's that got to do with Betty and him?"

"He minimized Dianna's absence, when she clearly only visited them on special occasions, something that hurt and infuriated Betty."

"How do figure that?"

"When she said, 'She was never too busy to call *me*, Frank', there was a slight accent on '*me*', emphasizing that *he* was the reason Dianna didn't visit."

"Yeah, I heard that. But it didn't seem like such a big deal."

"That's because she spoke softly, Joe. She controlled her tone. But it was a shade *too* controlled, as if she might lose it. And there was a clear flash of A.U. nine." Julie pointed to her nose. "Her levator labii superioris …"

Joe held up his hand. "Hold it! In English, please."

"Sorry. I was referring to her facial expression. An 'A.U.' is a distinct movement of facial muscle, an 'Action Unit'. There are forty-three basic movements that work in combination with each other. In this case, the A.U. was a micro expression, Joe, something a person can't control. It was fleeting, barely noticeable, but I caught it.

"Betty scrunched her nose…*like this.* You know, the way you do when you smell something bad? Your eyebrows automatically lower at the same time, see? That's number nine, Joe. It's a universal expression of disgust. But that wasn't all. Generally, a person also lowers their eyelids. Betty didn't do that. She looked straight at Frank, open-eyed. That was pure, undiluted anger."

"Hmm, that's interesting," said Joe. "She never says much, but, now that you mention it, it fits with something else I thought about in there. Maybe she didn't *want* to move to Florida. Maybe she blames him for that. Like maybe Dianna would still be alive if they never moved here. I mean, it doesn't have to make sense for her to feel like that, right?"

"I think you're right. And Frank was clearly disingenuous about the move. I think Betty wasn't the only one who probably felt uprooted. What was Dianna, seventeen or eighteen? I'd be willing to bet that she didn't want to move here, either."

They were quiet for a few moments, as they each thought about the Wielands.

The community's exit gate rose slowly as they approached.

"Well, it's only noon, Merlin," said Joe, pulling over to the curb.

"Who's next on your list?"

6

"Okay, Linc, thanks. We'll see you then."

Joe slipped the cell phone into its dashboard holster.

"He can't meet us until four. He's tied up at work until then. He works at Pleasure Ride Farm, near Ocala. It's beautiful, Merlin. You'll enjoy seeing it."

"Good. Let's see if we can catch Lee Porter at Porter & Brandt. I'd rather not call. I've learned from experience that it's better not to give an attorney a heads-up. Besides, if he's not there we can still talk to his secretary."

Porter & Brandt was one of the largest and oldest law firms in the area, occupying its own building on New York Avenue, one block east of trendy Park Avenue in Winter Park. The handsome Spanish architecture of stucco and tile had aged well, and fit right in with the overall ambiance of older homes and bricked streets.

As Julie and Joe entered, they could see that major renovations were underway inside. Large, clear plastic sheets were strung across the lobby and workmen were noisily knocking down a wall behind it. A receptionist with headphones was sitting at a circular desk. She removed them as they approached.

"Hi," said Joe, his voice raised over the ruckus. "We're here to see Lee Porter, is he in?"

"Do you have an appointment?" she said, enunciating carefully.

"No. Would you tell him it's Joe Garrett? It's important."

"One minute, please," she said, holding up a finger and mouthing the words as if they needed to read her lips. They listened while she loudly relayed the information. A few moments later she said in the same exaggerated, gesticulating way, "Mr. Porter is in court, but Evelyn, his secretary will be right out." She motioned them toward a bank of leather chairs.

Julie and Joe shared a smile as they turned and took a seat.

Evelyn Hoag joined them almost immediately and Julie remembered her as soon as she saw her. She was in her thirties, attractive in a healthy, athletic way. Her brown hair was cut straight and curved to the line of her jaw, framing large, intelligent eyes. One could picture her leading an exercise class, or organizing a mini-marathon for charity.

She sat close so they could hear her, apologizing for Lee Porter's absence and for the noise.

"Is there anything I can help you with?"

Julie explained what they were doing, and Evelyn, who was obviously fond of Dianna, was eager to talk to them. "Come on back to the office where we can talk."

They followed her down a long hallway to Lee Porter's office which looked out on a picturesque garden area with a fountain. Evelyn's smaller, adjoining office had the same lovely view. When the door closed behind them, the noise from the front was muffled and minimal.

"Please, have a seat," she said, motioning them to join her at a small round table. "I can't tell you how much I miss Dianna! We were good friends. I'm still in shock over what happened. How can I help you?"

There wasn't the slightest doubt that she was sincere. Sadness had overtaken her features and her eyes glistened with held-back tears.

"You knew her well?" asked Julie.

"Yes. Many years. We handled all Bay Street Realty's commercial transactions, some residential, as well. Dianna and I became quite close. We talked regularly on the phone and met for lunch. We went out for dinner together just recently…"

Their last supper…her voice caught and she squeezed her eyes shut tightly.

———

As usual, Evelyn had noticed several male heads turn as Dianna left her seat at the bar to follow the hostess to their table on the outside patio. Then the waiter who came to take their order couldn't tear his eyes away from her, either.

It was always that way. Evelyn didn't blame them, though. How could she?

"Oh, no," said Dianna. "He's coming over."

Evelyn turned and saw a blond guy, who had sent them drinks at the bar, making his way toward them, waving and smiling. He pulled up a chair, said "Excuse me," to Evelyn and immediately commenced talking to Dianna. She listened politely to his non-stop monologue, waiting for him to take a breath so she could get a word in. Finally, she got the opportunity when the waiter arrived and interrupted him.

"You really shouldn't have sent us drinks, Hal. I think I told you I have a boyfriend, but thanks for stopping by. Have a good evening," she said.

Crestfallen, the man got up and retreated to his group at the bar.

"I apologize, Evelyn. Some people are just so rude you can't be nice to them."

Evelyn had been unable to restrain herself.

"How does it feel to be so beautiful that you mesmerize everyone who sees you?"

Dianna had blushed scarlet.

"Me? You must be kidding!"

And she actually meant it…

The tears fell now, despite Evelyn's effort to control them.

"Evelyn? Are you alright?" asked Julie.

"Yes. Excuse me," she said, grabbing Kleenex from a box on her desk. "I haven't gotten over this yet. It's just too terrible."

This woman is grieving; she needs to talk about Dianna.

"What can you tell us about her, Evelyn?"

"She was beautiful…mesmerizing…but completely unassuming. I don't think she realized the effect she had on people. But Dianna was beautiful on the inside, too. She was vibrant and funny and warm. We had such good times together." She sighed. "She was very smart, too. Maybe a little naïve…"

"Naïve? In what way?"

"Oh, she was an optimist, that's all. She believed in happy endings."

"That doesn't sound very suicidal," said Joe.

"No. That's the whole thing…she *wasn't* like that. I can't believe she did that!"

Her face crumpled.

Julie quickly reached out and covered Evelyn's hand with her own. "Obviously, she meant a lot to you. If it's any comfort, Evelyn, I don't believe it, either."

Unsure of where to go from there, Julie was glad that Joe intervened and changed the direction of the conversation.

"Evelyn, do you happen to recall a 'letter of complaint' that was filed against Bay Street Realty?"

"Ah, let me think," she said, withdrawing her hand from Julie, momentarily resting her chin on her hand. Her index finger rubbed along the side of her nose.

"Lee may know something about that. He'll be here later today. Do you want to come back?"

"No, we can't today," said Joe, "we're headed up to Ocala." He stood up and so did Julie. "Just tell him we'd like to talk to him about it, if he can. One of us will call tomorrow, okay?"

"Of course, I'll tell him you stopped by."

They both thanked her, and she walked them out to the lobby, where workers had disappeared and the din of remodeling had abated.

They were getting into the Land Rover when Joe asked Julie a question.

"The nose thing, when I asked her about the complaint, was she lying?"

"I don't think so, Joe. Sometimes a person just has an itchy nose, you know," said Julie, smiling. "Seriously, though, I think it *was* significant. Up until then, her posture was open and she was leaning forward. She sat back and closed up slightly when you asked that question. But I'm thinking it was a *secretary's* reaction. I think your question went beyond her personal feelings…and into Lee Porter's business."

"So she was dodging the question, right?"

"No, not dodging. She wanted us to come back *today*. She wanted Lee Porter to tell us. I believe Evelyn Hoag wants to help us in every possible way, Joe. What she felt for Dianna was more than friendship."

"But Dianna didn't…"

"No…probably not."

7

~

The countryside flew by as Julie looked out the window of the Land Rover. Nothing in the passing landscape itself said *cold*. Flat land had given way to green, gently rolling pastures dotted with massive Century oaks and stands of palm, all of it bathed in brilliant afternoon sunshine. The land was stoic in the face of the frigid air that swept down overnight from the North. It lay in wait, trusting in the power of the Florida sun to eventually warm things up. But the behavior of cows gave away the breezy, mid-fifties temperature. Usually, they were grazing or reclining under the trees in a loose cluster, shaded from the hot afternoon sun. But today, as Julie and Joe sped by on the turnpike, small groups stood in the sunshine, black and white bodies pressed together, as if enclosed by invisible pens.

"Do they leave the cows out all night when it's this cold, Joe?"

"Cattle? Sure. I'm not sure about dairy cows. They take horses in, though."

"So what exactly does Lincoln Tyler do at Pleasure Ride Farm?"

"He's a hired hand, basically. Lives in a cottage on the property, tends to the horses and works wherever they need him. Lincoln's real interest is rodeo competition. He's won some all-around cowboy championships in the International Pro-Rodeo Association."

Joe was on I-75 now, and Julie noticed the marked difference in the land as the hills became more pronounced. Still, it sure didn't look like cowboy country.

"I just don't think of Florida when I think of cowboys," she said. "Maybe it's because I'm from the northeast. Everything I know about horses and cattle comes from western movies."

"I know," said Joe. "Most people don't. It's funny, because it all started here. Ponce de Leon brought the horses, and the cattle, too. Hundreds of years ago, the Florida Panhandle had dozens of cattle ranches. In fact, Texas Longhorn cattle are descendants. The Seminole Indians and the settlers had herds, too, all over the state. So, when the railroads came, Florida was all set to become a major beef and leather supplier for the Confederacy. After the civil war, the state became a supplier for the whole country. It's a *huge* business in Florida.

"But you're right, it's different here. There's not a lot of fenced pasture. The big herds are mostly on open range all the way down to Lake Okeechobee. It's a challenge for cowboys, Julie. They have to round them up over miles of open plain, rivers, hammocks and swamp. You ask me, I think it's a *lot* easier to be a cowboy out west."

He took an exit and they were on a two-lane country road, lined on both sides with wood corral fencing. Julie spotted a few horses as they drove along. After a few minutes, they saw a green and black sign rimmed in gold: *Pleasure Ride Farm.* A matching green and black arch with the circled brand *PR* spanned the entrance. Joe slowed and turned right onto a long, red dirt road.

The pastures were lush with giant trees, many hung with lacy hems of Spanish moss. It was late afternoon and their long shadows striped the lawns with every shade of green and gold. The horses were more plentiful here, some right along the fence. Julie was tempted to ask him to stop so she could pet them. Feeling childish, she kept that to herself.

"You were right, Joe. This *is* a beautiful farm."

They passed a white stable with green and black trim, where some horses and riders were gathered. Considering the time of day, Julie thought they must be returning from a trail ride. Ahead of them sprawled a white ranch house with black shutters and a green door.

"Lincoln's cottage is past the main house, near the barn, over there," said Joe.

Rather than park out in front of the ten-stall barn, he swung around to the side. Julie could see Lincoln Tyler's cottage off to the right. Like all the buildings, it was painted white with green and black trim. On the left, the west-facing doors to the barn stood open, allowing the late afternoon sun to pour in.

"C'mon," said Joe.

Julie followed him inside. The uneven, well worn floor was covered with bits of straw and dirt, and the smell of horses, hay and leather was heady. It was earthy and satisfying. They walked down the center, all the way to the end, admiring the animals in their stalls. Julie finally succumbed to her inner horse-lover and stopped to stroke the velvety, golden nose of a curious palomino mare.

The slow clip-clop of a horse entering the barn caught their attention and they turned. The horse and the man leading him were dark figures, starkly silhouetted by the brilliant sun.

"Hello, Mr. Garrett."

As he neared and her eyes adjusted, Julie caught her breath.

He looks just like James Dean. Well worth a trip to Ocala, Dianna.

"Hi, Linc," said Joe. "This is my friend, Julie O'Hara. Julie, this is Lincoln Tyler."

"Linc," he said, sticking out his hand.

He's not young. Not old, either; early thirties maybe? Even his mannerisms are like Dean's; the off-center smile, the shy, downward glance.

"Just give me a minute," he said, "'til I get him settled in."

He led the big chestnut stallion into his stall and

removed the horse's blanket. A couple of pats on the horse's back and he latched the gate.

"Let's go in here," he said, leading the way to a tack room off the center of the barn.

It was a spacious room, surprisingly warm and comfortable. A scarred oak desk and three chairs, black leather cushions tied to the seats, were on the right. Saddles and bridles hung on pegs over a long bench on the left wall, while closed cabinets covered the far wall. Julie was surprised by the relative neatness of it all.

Linc plopped into the chair behind the desk.

"So, how you like Pleasure Ride, Ms. O'Hara?"

The double entendre was not lost on her.

"It's beautiful, Linc. You can probably tell I love horses."

"Yep. Do you ride?"

"When I was a kid," said Julie, smiling as she remembered.

"You should come back. We got some great trails in the Ocala National Forest and the Greenway. You can go half-day or all day."

"Now I'm feeling left out, Linc," said Joe. "You didn't ask *me* to come back."

Both men laughed, and Linc said, "You already came back, Mr. Garrett."

Lincoln invites female attention; it's different, though, somehow. It's almost as if he's doing it to validate his own masculinity.

"Did Dianna ride, Linc?" she asked.

It was comedy to tragedy. Like a clown smiling and passing a hand down over his face, Lincoln's features were suddenly pulled downward. His misery was palpable.

"Yeah, she did."

"Did she come up here to ride? Is that how you met?"

"No," he said, "we met last year, in February."

His eyes drifted aside, as if he were remembering.

"It was at the Silver Spurs Rodeo …"

"Cowboy up!"

The gate swung open and instantly Linc's focus narrowed to the rhythm and swing of the bull. The pulsing of his own blood drowned out the roar of the rodeo fans in the Silver Spurs Arena. Black Lightning was two-thousand pounds of pissed-off fury, determined to rid himself of the weight on his back. Linc held onto the braided rope with a single gloved hand, his other arm whipping around for balance on the furious, spinning bull.

Addicted to the danger of bull-riding, Linc craved the adrenalin rush. When it coursed through him, the brief ride became a slow-motion high where his seat and control were perfect. He gloried in it for stretched-out seconds, and then dismounted cleanly on the outside of a spin.

The pick-up rider swung Linc up behind him on his horse, while the nearest bullfighter, a clown in a barrel, emerged to distract the angry bull. Linc, exhilarated, waved to the crowd as they cantered away. Just before the exit, he thanked the pick-up and jumped off.

Dianna was there, right behind the rail. She had on low-rider jeans and a body-hugging red jersey. Her blue-green eyes were fringed with dark lashes, her skin the color of cream. She leaned over the railing, sweeping her dark hair away from her eyes.

They were meant for each other.

He called her that night and asked her to come to Pleasure Ride Farm. Mid-week had been best for both of them, since the weekends were busy. She arrived late Tuesday morning...and left on Wednesday. They'd gone riding in the forest, and planned to have dinner afterwards at Chili's. Neither of them said anything about staying the night. They didn't have to; it was a foregone conclusion.

They made love all night...on the floor in front of the fireplace, in his bed, in the shower. He'd been through hell and back in his life, but none of it mattered as long as he had Dianna.

Ten times she came to Pleasure Ride. And then she stopped.

"Lincoln? I was asking when you saw her last?"

"Oh, yeah, I'm sorry. It was after Thanksgiving, the first week of December, I think. Dianna came up every once in awhile, but, like I told Mr. Garrett, we weren't serious."

"Was she depressed or despondent about anything, Linc?"

"Not when I saw her, but that was two months before she…you know…"

"But you two talked on the phone during that time, right?" asked Joe. "She might have mentioned something, been upset about something…"

"No. We didn't have much contact after December." He shifted in his seat, leaning forward, his forearms on his legs. His head was tilted down, but his eyes were looking up at them. It was vintage James Dean; the real Linc had disappeared. "I don't know what else I can tell you. I sure hope you don't feel you wasted your time coming up here."

"Not at all," said Julie, standing up, reaching across the desk to shake his hand. "Thanks for your time, Linc. It was nice to meet you, and a pleasure to see Pleasure Ride."

"The pleasure was mine," Lincoln drawled, half-smile back in place.

"Thanks again, Linc," said Joe.

⁓

"Did the police investigate Lincoln, Joe?"

"Yeah, they did. He was transporting a thoroughbred to Gulfstream Park."

"That's a racetrack, right? Where is it?"

"It's in Hallandale, between Fort Lauderdale and Miami. Linc delivered the horse the night before Dianna died and said he stayed the next morning to watch the workout," said Joe.

"Did anybody see him there?" asked Julie.

"The trainer said he always stayed to watch."

"That's not the same thing as saying specifically, '*I saw him there that morning*'."

"I know, but Detective McPhee is 'satisfied' with Linc's alibi, and I'm quoting," said Joe. "If we want anymore on that we'll have to get it ourselves."

"Maybe we should," said Julie.

They rode in silence for awhile.

"So, what do you think?" said Joe. "Was it worth the ride up here, apart from the scenery?"

"Yes, it was. He's an interesting guy. Hard to read, though. He's a man who's learned to control his expressions."

"He looks like Jimmy Dean, huh?" said Joe, glancing at her with a tinge of jealousy.

"James Dean. Yes, he does," said Julie impassively.

"He's probably been told that many times. He plays the part because it works for him. Anyway," she said, "that makes him hard to read. But I think you were right. Dianna was from a different social milieu. For some reason, she hadn't been up to Pleasure Ride Farm for almost two months, and that's a long time for lovers. Maybe she decided to stop seeing him. Maybe Lincoln cared for her more than she cared for him. That would be hard for someone like him to take…harder than he's willing to admit."

"He really looked miserable when you first mentioned her name, though."

"Yes, he did…but was it grief?"

8

The phone beside her bed was ringing insistently. Julie wanted to disconnect it, but she was too tired. She opened her eyes slightly. It was pitch dark out! Sol was even asleep, upside down on the bottom of the bed, feet in the air. Who had the *nerve* to call in the middle of the night?

"Hello…who is this?" she said.

"It's me, sleepyhead," said Joe. "Time to get up. I'll be there in a half-hour."

"What? No. It's too early."

"No, it's not. We *need* to be early if we want to catch the trainer at Gulfstream."

"Oh, *all right*! I'm getting up."

Fortified with coffee and doughnuts, Julie felt a lot better. She had dressed appropriately in jeans and low boots, not knowing exactly where they might be walking at Gulfstream Park. The sun was climbing in the east and the Land Rover was chewing up the Florida Turnpike between Orlando and the Southeast Florida coast. They'd been going over the questions they planned to ask and had decided that Joe would take the lead this time. Julie was thinking they'd be at Gulfstream Park in another half-hour or so, when Joe suddenly pulled to the right and got on an exit ramp.

"We're getting off here? I thought the track was further south, in Hallandale."

"Gulfstream Park *is* in Hallandale," said Joe, taking the Boynton Beach exit off the Florida Turnpike. "We're going to Palm Meadows Thoroughbred Training Center. That's where Lincoln Tyler actually took Beau Grande, the colt he was transporting. Beau Grande ran in the second race February 4th at Gulfstream, but he trained for it here at Palm Meadows. Jack Folsom, Beau Grande's trainer, was already here waiting for Linc to deliver the horse. That's the guy we're going to see."

"So, he's the one McPhee spoke with?"

"Yes. He said to go in the second entrance and they'd direct us to the barn."

They turned in and were surprised to discover that the stable area consisted of *forty* barns! And they were *big*, with thirty-six stalls each. Palm Meadows was three-hundred plus landscaped acres with a grid of horse paths connecting all the barns to a track. It was a state-of-the-art facility where thoroughbreds were never subjected to pavement. For the uninitiated, however, it was a dirt path maze. Fortunately, they were given a map with directions to barn ten, stall twenty-two, where they hoped to find Jack Folsom.

If they were two minutes later, they would have missed him.

There was a commotion outside stall twenty-two. A jockey was mounting "Pair-O-Dice"- a huge, dark-chocolate horse with a double diamond blaze on his forehead. The excited animal couldn't seem to stand still. The trainer led the horse forward a few feet and settled him down. Folsom had short, dark hair parted nearly in the middle and a sinewy strength about him that reminded Julie of the boxers of yesteryear.

"Hi," he said, turning toward them, "Joe Garrett?"

"Yep. You must be Mr. Folsom," said Joe. "This is Julie O'Hara."

They all shook hands.

"Call me Jack. Nice to meet you. This is Carlos," he said, indicating the jockey, who smiled, acknowledging them. "We're headed to the track. Pair-O-Dice is breezing today and we don't have a lot of time. Do you mind talking while we walk?"

"No, not at all," said Joe as they fell in step next to him.

"Did you say 'breezing'?" asked Julie. "I don't believe I've ever heard that term; what does it mean?"

"Pair-O-Dice has been doing slow gallops for the last few days. Today he'll 'breeze' at racing speed. The turf track is only open for breezing for an hour, so we need to get right over there," he said. "You wanted to talk to me about Beau Grande and Linc Tyler?"

"Yes," said Joe. "Beau Grande came down on the twenty-seventh of January to train for the race on February fourth. Do you remember *when* he arrived that day?"

"It was around dinner time, five or six o'clock. I remember because I was tired and I wanted to go eat, but I had to wait for Beau Grande."

"Did Lincoln leave after turning the horse over to you?" asked Julie.

"No, he helped me get Beau Grande settled in for the night, and then we left."

"You went out to eat?"

"Nah, I was too beat. I went back to the pavilion here at Palm Meadows. I'm leasing a one-bedroom apartment for the season. I invited Linc to come over for a sandwich and a beer, told him he could sleep on the couch if he wanted to, but he said he was all set, he had a room at the Best Western. Didn't blame him. That's a long ride for a sandwich and a couch."

Pair-O-Dice snorted and started dancing around again.

"Almost there, boy, almost there," soothed the trainer, picking up the pace a bit. The horse calmed down almost immediately and they resumed their walk.

"Sorry," said Folsom. "Pair-O-Dice loves to run. He senses it when we're gonna let him go; makes him antsy. What did you ask me?"

"I was asking if Lincoln Tyler was here the next morning," said Joe.

"Oh, yeah. Linc always comes by first thing in the morning to watch. I usually have the jockey pick it up down the stretch to see what kind of shape the horse is in. Lots of handicappers out here in the morning."

"What time would that be?" asked Julie.

"Six-thirty."

"So you saw Lincoln here?"

"Yeah, I'm pretty sure I did," said Folsom.

They had reached the track.

"Look, I'm sorry, but I can't talk to you guys anymore. I got a horse to run. I gotta get him out there *now*," said Folsom leading Pair-O-Dice onto the turf.

"No problem," called Joe after the trainer. "Thanks! Good luck in the race!"

"Well, it wasn't a total waste," said Joe, as they walked back to the Land Rover. "Pair-O-Dice looks like a good bet."

"What about the Best Western?" asked Julie.

"McPhee already confirmed that Linc checked in there that night. Of course, there's no way to know when he left."

"I don't think Folsom knows if Lincoln Tyler was here that morning or not," said Julie. "I don't pretend to be able to read someone's body language while they're leading a skittish horse. Still, for my money, I think he's standing up for Linc, giving him the benefit-of-the-doubt out of friendship."

"Yeah, I'd put my money on that one, too."

"You know what else, Joe? Maybe Folsom *couldn't*

see everybody hanging around the track that day. I know for a fact that at six-thirty that morning in Orlando it was *dark and foggy.* What are the odds it was like that here?"

"Better than Pair-O-Dice," said Joe.

9

At exactly quarter past four on Thursday, Julie stepped into the law office of Porter & Brandt for her solo meeting with Lee Porter. She recalled the last time she had seen him, all decked out in a tuxedo. Could it be that he looked even better in a regular suit? Due to good genes and money, Lee Porter was younger looking than his forty-five years. He was about six feet tall and fit, thanks to a tennis club membership. His dark hair was shot through with silver-gray.

He rose from his desk to shake her hand.

"Hello, Ms. O'Hara, I'm Lee Porter. What can I do for you?"

"Please call me Julie. Actually, we've met before...at a charity event...the Black and White Ball? Your wife, Sylvia, introduced us, although she may have used my business name, 'Merlin'." Julie reached into a side pocket of her purse and handed him a card.

"Oh, of course!" he said, hitting his forehead in a classic 'boy-am-I-dumb' gesture. "I believe we've seen each other at the courthouse, too. You were working with John Tate. Sorry, Julie. I didn't connect the names."

"No apology necessary," said Julie with a chuckle. "It's not the first time."

"So…Evelyn told me you came by a couple days ago with Joe Garrett?"

"Yes. You know that Joe is working for Frank and Betty Wieland, looking into the circumstances of their daughter's death. I live next to Lake Eola, Lee. I was there the morning they found her. Suffice to say that I signed on to help her parents get some closure."

Lee sat back with his arms loosely crossed, a guarded gesture.

"So…what can I do for you?"

Julie figured that Evelyn had told him about their inquiry regarding the letter. She plowed ahead, presuming it had gone to the Florida Real Estate Commission.

"I understand there was a letter about Bay Street Realty sent to FREC. Do you recall the particulars of the complaint?"

Lee visibly relaxed, unconsciously unbuttoning his jacket and leaning forward.

"Yes. Yes, I do. That was Mike Menello, a contractor. He got caught up in building spec houses during the boom. He paid top dollar for three lakefront lots in Quill Creek. Built two McMansions before the bottom fell out of the market."

"Did he lose them?"

"Oh, yes," he said, his brow furrowed in thought, his chin in his hand. "He went belly-up, lost everything. Even his own house, I think, which was mortgaged to the hilt. He blamed the seller for inflating the price of the lots, accused him of conspiring with the appraiser. Of course it wasn't true. Everything was inflated back then."

"How long ago was that, do you remember?"

"Nine, ten months ago."

"The seller listed with Bay Street Realty," said Julie.

Lee nodded, concern written on his face.

"Yes…and Dianna was his agent."

As Julie fought the evening traffic on her way back to her condo, she was consumed with curiosity about this man, Mike Menello.

Financial disaster had driven a lot of people to commit desperate acts. What kind of a person was he? Could he have blown this incident with Dianna out of all proportion and lost it? Julie wondered what possible excuse she could drum up to meet with the man. She was definitely going to run this by Joe.

She wished she had more time to devote to their investigation. She was still working on the revision of her book, *Clues.* The manuscript was, in fact, beside her in her briefcase. It would consume her evening and, no doubt, some of tomorrow. Although she had plans to have dinner with Joe tomorrow night, she decided to call him as soon as she got home to tell him about this guy.

Could the contractor have killed Dianna?

10

He sat with his head in his hands, running them through his hair, massaging his temples. How could he have been so stupid to have gone back there in the morning? Frustration from the night before, that's what it was. It came back to him with crystal clarity, the terrible consequences having seared every detail into his brain.

He had been driving slowly through her darkened Bay Hill neighborhood once again, circling, keeping watch on her townhouse. There was nowhere to park the SUV where he could keep the house in view and not be noticed. It was getting late, after ten o'clock, and he was about ready to give it up. He had to get up early the next day.

Just as the townhouse came into sight again, she came out and got into her car. His heartbeat quickened, and he sucked in his breath as he felt himself hardening. The white Lexus pulled out onto Apopka-Vineland Road.

He had followed discretely, a couple cars behind. When she headed for Interstate 4, he'd known exactly where she was going. She was headed to Lake Eola again, to the condo. She would drive down the side street and turn into the residents' parking lot behind the building. He was throbbing, beyond excited. It was payback time.

How could you do that to me, you bitch?

He'd pulled into the passing lane on I-4 and floored it.

Franklin was a quiet street, lined with big trees. He would get there before her. He thought about the knife in the glove compartment. It was late and dark behind that building. It would only take a minute or two. He would force her into the SUV.

Exiting I-4 into the Downtown area, he'd taken Rosalind Ave north to East Robinson and turned left onto the familiar street. He passed the condo building with its tiered balconies, and turned into the darkened parking lot, backing into a space that gave him a clear view of the entrance. Invisible behind the tinted glass, he'd waited, stroking himself.

It wasn't a long wait. The Lexus made the turn into Franklin and slowed to a near stop at the entrance to the parking lot...a moment passed...and she continued on up the street.

What the hell was she doing?

And then he'd understood. She thought the parking

lot was full! She couldn't see the couple remaining spaces to his left. Quickly, he followed her, just in time to see the Lexus turn right at the intersection. She was headed around the block, probably looking for a parking space.

She had turned right onto East Robinson once again. She passed Franklin and quickly pulled left into a small parking area on the other side of the street, next to the lake. He pulled into the next driveway, the Eola Park Center parking lot. He wasn't six feet from her, across a narrow, down-sloping strip of grass. He grabbed the knife, flicked it open and started to get out, glancing behind them. Cars were passing intermittently on the busy street.

Fuming, he whacked the knife closed, nicking his palm in the process.

He'd sat there helplessly as she darted across the road, ran up the steps of the condo and let herself in.

———

He never should have gone back that morning, but he couldn't help himself, couldn't think of anything else. He didn't want to kill her. It just got out of hand because he was so hot and angry. Okay, maybe he did want to kill her for a while there. But he didn't *plan* to do that. He just wanted to make her suffer for what she did.

Her getting cut was an accident, for Christ's sake, a stupid accident.

He would not give himself away; he would not panic and run. He couldn't outrun a *murder* charge. They'd hunt him for the rest of his life, find him wherever he went. No, he would not do that. He had to keep acting as if nothing at all had happened.

And he was, by now, a consummate actor.

11

I t was Friday night, and popular Thornton Park on the east side of Lake Eola was coming alive as the dusk deepened, as it did every evening when the weather was good. The older Downtown area had been rehabilitated and was developing a whole new cachet with the opening of boutique shops and bistro-style restaurants. Julie and Joe were on their way to grab a burger at Graffiti Junktion, a new favorite.

"Look, there's LatZero, Joe. Let's see what's going on."

Latitude Zero was an art gallery, the first to open in Thornton Park. It was a venue for multiple art forms; cartoons, photography, painting and sculpture, to name a few.

"Rats! No performance art tonight," she said.

Julie had toiled all day in the office catching up on things, and she was longing for some diversionary entertainment. They browsed around the gallery, stopping to admire a couple of riotously colorful paintings.

"These remind me of Marc's work," she said wistfully. "I wonder how David's doing with the gallery in Key West. I should call him."

Julie's good friend, Marc Solomon, a prominent artist, had died two years prior. His paintings of Key West were on permanent display there in the Sandpiper Gallery managed by their mutual friend, David Harris.

"David's good. I saw him last month," said Joe.

Julie looked at him, surprised.

"I guess I didn't tell you. I went down to do some diving with Will Sawyer," he said, "I just needed to get away for awhile."

So that's where you disappeared to.

"Let's go eat," said Joe, changing the subject. "I went back to the Medical Examiner, the Parks Department and the Orlando police today. I brought them up to speed on our investigation, but they didn't have anything new for us. I did see Detective McPhee, though. I want to tell you what I found out about that contractor, Menello."

Graffiti Junktion, casual dining on steroids, was already crowded. An irresistible mix of sports bar and train station, its big, happy bar and picnic tables were covered with fantastic graffiti. A small, outside table opened up and they made a bee-line for it.

They ordered their favorite burgers and a double order of Chef Tom's zucchini fries, a sinful delight masquerading as a vegetable. Julie sipped gratefully on a scotch and soda, while Joe, a recovering alcoholic, stuck with a coke. He had no idea how much she admired him for that. She would have told him, but she knew he didn't want to make a big deal out of it.

"Lee Porter was right," said Joe, leaning forward to keep their conversation as private as possible. "Mike Menello hates Bay Street Realty and particularly had it in for Dianna Wieland. The guy's a young hotshot. His father was a contractor like mine, so he grew up in the business. He put a pitch on his father and Daddy staked him for the deposit on the three lakefront lots in Quill Creek. But, off the record, McPhee says the guy's an asshole. He was in over his head, paid too much for everything, not just the lots. The subcontractors took him to the cleaners…no loyalty to Daddy, I guess."

"Oh, my God," said Julie. "He had *motive*, Joe."

"Yeah, but he also had an alibi. A girlfriend swore that he was with her from eleven the night before until nine o'clock that morning."

"C'mon…he could have sneaked out!"

"She lives near Disney in Windsor Place, twenty miles away from here," said Joe. "It's a gated community. He could have left easy enough, but getting back in without her knowing about it would have been tough."

"It's not *that* tough. You just wait for a car to go in and follow behind."

"People are going *out* in the early morning, Merlin. Not so many going in. A car hanging around like that might have a long wait. Look, you're reaching for straws. This isn't like you."

Julie sighed. "I know. I feel emotionally connected to Dianna. I can't sleep; I dream about her, Joe. I don't know how to explain it. I feel *pressed* to find her killer. She didn't do it. I know she didn't."

His hand covered hers. "Stay with me tonight, Julie. You're going at this twenty-four-seven. Take tonight off…you'll sleep better."

"We'll sleep?"

"Sure. After."

———

Hmmm…what a difference a good night's sleep can make.

The shower felt wonderful. Julie felt wonderful.

Mr. Wonderful was shaving.

"Should we go downstairs together and make their day?" asked Joe.

"No. I can't stand it. They make me feel like I'm in a soap opera."

"Whereas, you're just in *soap*," said Joe, pulling back the shower curtain, planting a kiss on her shoulder. "Want the razor?"

"Yes, thank you. You know what? Let's do this…you go downstairs first and call me if the coast is clear. I have to go home to feed Sol and change my clothes, and then I'll come back."

"Okay. It's early. They won't be in yet."

With a big grin, he took her face in his hands and kissed her for real.

"See you later," he said and closed the curtain.

It almost worked.

Julie got down the stairs, out the door and on her scooter before Luz pulled into the parking lot and waved. Sheepishly, she waved back, cursing her timing. She would *not* explain anything, no matter how Luz might bring it up.

That would only feed the fire...

When she unlocked her apartment door a few minutes later, Sol was right there. The beautiful Bengal cat rubbed against her knees, relieved to see her. Julie surveyed the mess he had made entertaining himself in her absence. There wasn't any real damage...

The cat had knocked her plastic mug stuffed with pens and pencils off her desk again. They were widely scattered over the spacious living room. Some were pushed off the oriental carpet, across the mahogany floor, as if he'd been playing with them. Julie loved her contemporary glass desk, but its clean lines only allowed for a retractable computer keyboard. At moments like this, she sorely missed a drawer in which to stash the pens and pencils. She thought about putting them high up in the bookcase.

No. It doesn't matter. He'll get them. He'll knock everything down.

She sighed with resignation and threw open the

French doors to let in some air and let the sleek, exotic cat out. Sol immediately tore around to the left side of the building. The large wraparound balcony housed his custom-built litter box. Only in dire emergency would the proud cat use the doggie-door she had installed nearby.

Julie picked up the scattered pens and pencils, and replaced the mug on the desk, wedging it in between the computer monitor and the modem. Then she went into her bedroom. As she changed her clothes, she thought about Joe…and Dan.

I love Joe. I do. But I don't want to get married again.

Thoughts of her husband, Dan O'Hara, came back, filling Julie with an emptiness that knew no bottom. It was strange how, even loving Joe, she still missed Dan.

He was my first love… my forever love.

So very many years ago…Julie was only twenty when they met. It was in Boston. She had been hired as a salesperson at an automobile dealership.

Julie smiled, thinking back on that.

It really was *a big deal, back then. There weren't many other women selling cars.*

It had been going so well until Dan showed up.

His picture could have been in the dictionary next to "chauvinist"…but it also could have been next to "Superman". Her friend, Marc, had said Dan looked like Superman…and he *did*. He was tall and strong, and he had the same wavy dark hair…a lock of which always fell across his forehead.

Theirs had been a charged relationship from the

very beginning. They started out as implacable enemies, but they were destined for the other side of the coin, and they became the most passionate of lovers.

Those were the days when people who had sex got married.

How times had changed. Still, Julie would have married Dan no matter what the mores of the time…a hundred years ago…a hundred years from now.

Daniel Patrick O'Hara had died on their honeymoon.

It happened on an idyllic Caribbean island in the Abacos chain called Castle Cay. Julie and Dan had sunned and played and made love. They became *one*. Then half of them got caught in a deadly rip tide and the other half tried to save him…and failed.

For many years, she'd had nightmares about drowning. Joe had helped her overcome that. And he had given her the courage to love again, too. But Julie didn't have enough courage to marry. Part of her had died with Dan. What if she married Joe and lost him? Would anything be left?

Sol came loping into the bedroom and Julie forced the introspection out of her head.

"Hello, Handsome," she said. "It's just you and me, buddy."

The cat, prone to vocalizing, replied with an enthusiastic meow.

Julie laughed out loud.

In her wildest dreams she couldn't imagine Joe living with Sol, anyway.

12

~~~

The weather was delightful, and Julie reluctantly locked her scooter and climbed into Joe's Land Rover for the ride to southwest Orlando. They were headed for an area the locals referred to simply as "Dr. Phillips". It was a name attached to a shopping area, a park, a neighborhood and a hospital, to name a few of the good doctor's philanthropies.

They had arranged to see Barry Costello, Dianna Wieland's personal trainer, and Sabrina Nolen of the Nolen Title Agency, which handled nearly all of Bay Street Realty's residential closings.

Sabrina Nolen, both Dianna's friend and a business associate, was first.

They sat in the reception area at Nolen Title in the Dr. Phillips Marketplace, waiting for Sabrina to wrap up an early closing. Joe was reading USA Today and Julie was looking through magazines when Sabrina emerged. She was a plump blonde in her mid to late thirties. Heavy makeup did little to hide an acne-like skin problem.

She was shaking hands and congratulating a young couple who were obviously first-time home owners. They were accompanied by a young man whom Julie assumed was their agent. As they left the office the couple thanked her effusively, and Sabrina promised to be at their beck and call, should they have any questions.

"Hello, Joe," she said, turning to them. "And you must be Julie O'Hara."

"Yes. Nice to meet you, Sabrina."

"'Merlin', I believe! Your reputation precedes you, Julie. What an interesting profession!"

"Yes, it is that," said Julie.

"Well, come on in. We can talk in here."

She directed them to the end of an oval conference table with coffee and a half-empty plate of doughnuts. Sabrina helped herself to one as soon as she sat down.

"I still can't believe Dianna's *gone*," she said between delicate bites. "Every once in awhile, I come across her name on a transaction and it just stops me cold."

"You were friends as well as business associates?" asked Julie.

Sabrina momentarily looked down.

"Yes, we were," said Sabrina. "After my divorce we became good friends. Dianna was one of those people, just fun to be around. We went out together several times."

Past tense...a falling-out between them, even before Dianna's death?

"She was dating Lincoln Tyler from Ocala," said Julie. "Did you ever meet him?"

"Just the once," she said. "Dianna got it into her head to go to the Silver Spurs Rodeo in Kissimmee, and I went with her. She seemed fascinated by Linc Tyler from the beginning. She nearly fell over the railing trying to talk to him. A few days later she went up to Ocala."

"So you never went up there riding with her?" asked Joe.

"No," she said, laughing. "Dianna didn't need a girlfriend along for the ride."

"She stopped going up there in December," said Julie. "Did she tell you why, Sabrina?"

"Yes, she did. She said Linc was getting too serious. She said he came down and showed up at her house. For some reason, she didn't want to go out with him around here. It didn't really make that much sense to me. It wasn't like Dianna was a snob or anything. Anyhow, she broke up with him the next weekend when she went to Ocala. I remember her saying that she 'should have told him over the phone'."

"Did he get physical with her?" asked Joe.

"That was the impression I got, but she never said so."

"Do you know Mike Menello, Sabrina?" asked Julie.

Sabrina immediately sat back and crossed her arms.

"Yes, I do, he's a contractor. Why do you ask?"

"I understand there were some hard feelings between him and Bay Street Realty, specifically with Dianna," said Julie.

"That had nothing to do with my office. We didn't handle that," she said, getting up. "Well, is there anything else I can help you with?" She looked at her watch. "I have folks coming in for a closing in a few minutes."

"No. That's fine. Thank you for seeing us," said Julie.

Joe thanked her, too, and they left.

Julie buckled her seat belt and looked at Joe.

"Where was that Menello guy staying?"

"Where does he live?" asked Joe.

"*No*. Where was he the morning Dianna died?"

"Oh. Windsor Place. Up Apopka-Vineland Road."

"I know where it is. She lives on Windsor Place Drive," said Julie.

"Who does?"

"*Sabrina*. Her address was on the magazines."

They went to lunch at Press 101, a wine bar in the Marketplace, and mulled over the possibility that Sabrina Nolen could be Mike Menello's alibi. An hour later, they were walking into the Dr. Phillips Community YMCA.

"So Barry Costello never went to Dianna's townhouse?" asked Julie.

"No. She trained here with him twice a week," said Joe. "I don't think there was anything going on between *them*, though. That's him there, behind the desk."

"Hi, Barry," said Joe.

"Oh, hi, Mr. Garrett," said Barry, stepping out from behind the desk.

Julie hoped her face didn't register her shock. Barry Costello was in his early twenties. He had dark curly hair and the kind of fresh-faced, blushing good looks that make teenage girls swoon. He also had a metal leg from his left knee down, ending in a sneaker.

"This is my friend, Julie O'Hara," said Joe. "Julie, meet Barry Costello, trainer to the Stars… at least in Dr. Phillips. No kidding! Barry's the most popular trainer here."

If possible, Barry blushed some more, and led them down a corridor to the right.

"Do you mind if we talk here in the gym? I'm coaching a girls' basketball game here." He looked at his watch, "In twenty minutes."

"I won't take long, Barry," said Julie. "I know you've already talked to Joe. I'm just trying to get a deeper understanding about Dianna Wieland from the point of view of her friends."

"Sure, what do you want to know?"

"Tell me anything. What was special about her? What kind of person was she?"

"Well…everybody knows she was beautiful. But she wasn't vain. I mean, I don't remember Dianna ever fussing like some girls do." He looked at Joe. "You know how some girls just talk about their hair all the time?" Joe nodded, and Julie learned something new about men.

Barry continued.

"She was an art lover. She volunteered in our After School art program. Last March she helped with a trip to the Winter Park Sidewalk Art Festival and in November they took the kids to Fiesta in the Park at Lake Eola. She enjoyed the kids…said she wanted to have a daughter some day."

Julie shot a quick look at Joe.

"Did Dianna go Downtown to Lake Eola very often, Barry?"

"No, I don't think so…it was just for the art show."

Barry's eyebrows formed an upside-down V. The corners of his mouth pulled down and trembled. For a moment, Julie thought he might cry. With effort, he pulled himself together.

"She was just a good person. I know she worked hard and wanted to get ahead. I don't know what else to tell you."

Julie put out her right hand to shake his, and then covered it with her left.

"You've told us more than enough, Barry. Thank you. I'm sorry for your loss."

The young man simply nodded.

Meanwhile, young girls and their parents were drifting into the gym.

Joe, God bless him, changed the sadness of the moment by clapping Barry on the shoulder.

"Hey, man. Good luck with the game! Is your team ready?"

"You bet!" said Barry.

As they left the gym and turned down the hallway, Julie elbowed Joe.

"You could have *told* me about his disability."

"You said you didn't want any 'extra info'. You said you didn't want to 'prejudge'."

"Okay, I did," said Julie.

"He opened up more this time," said Joe. "I didn't know about the volunteer stuff. I guess she really liked being around the kids."

"Do you still think Dianna killed herself over an unwanted pregnancy?"

"No. Not over that or anything else," said Joe.

"I think she was murdered."

13

⌒

I t was half-past six and getting darker by the minute when Sabrina Nolen finally hit the garage door opener on her visor and pulled into her three-car garage in Windsor Place. For just a moment when the door began to rise she pictured the garage full, as it once was before her divorce. But the antique Chevy and the Camaro were no longer there, having been granted to her ex-husband, Don.

Don also ended up with half the equity in the house, but Sabrina had no complaints. Falling real estate values had made his share smaller and she had no difficulty buying him out. As for the title company, that cash cow was all hers…along with her six rental properties.

Unlike most people, Sabrina had few illusions about herself. She was minimally attractive, a little overweight and past her prime. She was also aware that her money couldn't buy love.

But at least I don't have to suffer old, inattentive fools.

And Mike Menello was none of those.

Sabrina parked her baby blue Jag next to Mike's SUV, careful to leave enough space between them, since he'd already tapped her car once with his driver-side door.

"Hey, Baby, welcome home," he said as she entered the expansive kitchen.

He was stirring a pot of tomato sauce on the stove.

Except for the lingering evidence of a once broken nose, Mike Menello had a classic Roman face and a sculpted body that women coveted and men envied. Unduly praised as a boy, at thirty he was a stud who thought the world owed him success.

He held out a wooden spoon of sauce for her to taste.

"I made you Puttanesca", he said, "just like my mother used to make."

Sabrina smiled, knowing the name translated to "whore's spaghetti".

She doubted the name fit his mother.

"Hmm…delicious."

"Sit. I'll get you some wine. Cab or Merlot?" he asked.

She opted for the Merlot and took a seat at a large granite table adorned with fresh flowers and candles. The sliding glass doors to the pool were opened wide and soft music was playing.

Mike had laid the table with attention to detail.

And not just the table…

Sabrina was eight years older than Mike and virtually supporting him. Because of that, he was kissing her ass, both literally and figuratively.

For a good while as they ate, Mike talked about a deal he was on the verge of putting together, no doubt hoping for some financial support.

And then it was her turn.

"So how was *your* day?" he asked.

In retrospect, she told him about her meeting with Joe Garrett and Julie O'Hara specifically to see how he would react. No matter what she'd told the police, the truth was that Sabrina couldn't have known whether or not Mike left and came back, or if he slept like a log beside her the whole night.

Sabrina was an insomniac who took maximum strength sleeping pills.

Her medication was so hypnotic she couldn't remember getting up to go to the bathroom, much less if Mike was on the other side of a California King-sized bed.

Mike put down his fork and stared at her.

"What did you tell them?"

"I told them I knew you. That was all."

Do I, Mike?

14

Of all people, Julie O'Hara, teaming up with that private eye!

His panic was mounting by the day. How long would it take before she figured it out? Every instinct said *run*. But he knew better than that. It didn't make sense to take off. They already questioned him and moved on. He wasn't a suspect.

He was letting his imagination get the best of him.

Why should I give up everything, my whole life?

The cops already talked to Dianna's family, her friends and everybody.

Nothing came of it.

No…Julie O'Hara was his only *real* problem.

15

For the better part of a week, the Wielands' case had been on the back burner while Julie and Joe handled other business. For Julie, it was hard to stay focused on her clients. More and more real to her, Dianna continued to cry out for help and for justice.

At last Julie was able to clear her schedule. She called Bay Street Realty and on the spur of the moment asked Kate Winslow to lunch. They planned to meet at a restaurant in Dr. Phillips at noon. She called Joe to tell him.

"Thanks a lot for including me," he said, clearly miffed at the "ladies only" meeting.

His pique was understandable. Julie apologized, explaining that she felt she could get more information, woman-to-woman.

He had come to agree and they planned to meet later. But now he was throwing a stumbling block in her path. He didn't want her to talk to Kate about the pregnancy.

Julie was exasperated.

"Kate Winslow had to know about it, Joe; two women,

friends who also work together? If Dianna knew she was pregnant, she would have told her," said Julie. "Look, this pregnancy issue is important. Whether or not Dianna *knew* is a vital piece of information."

"The Wielands don't want the pregnancy broadcast, Merlin. I told you they wanted to keep it under wraps. The coroner said it was so early Dianna 'might not have known'. Frank and Betty prefer to believe that…even if we don't."

"Joe, let's be real here. What I can't believe is the way everyone's side-stepping this critical issue! There's no such thing as *slightly* pregnant. I have to be able to bring it up with Kate Winslow. Yes, 'unwanted' pregnancies can trigger depression and suicide, but in this case it may have set her up for murder! Are we going to get to the bottom of this or not?"

He sighed, "All right. I know you're right. I didn't make any specific promises about it. If it helps this investigation, at the end of the day they'll forgive me."

"Of course they will. Losing a child to suicide is the ultimate guilt-trip. If we can prove that Dianna's death *wasn't* self-inflicted, it will ease the pain for Frank and Betty. And, Joe, that's what they really hired you for, isn't it?"

———

The noontime crowd at Too Jays Deli and Bakery hummed with muted conversation. Black and white photos from an earlier place and time adorned the stucco walls, and strategically placed greenery gave everyone a bit of privacy.

Julie thumbed through the menu tempted by the wafting aromas. She had already ordered a glass of chardonnay. It was her hope that doing so would encourage Kate Winslow to do the same.

As it happened, they knew each other in passing, which was why it had been so easy to set up this lunch. Julie had been a speaker at a business seminar several months earlier which Kate Winslow had attended. A picture of Kate in Bay Street Realty's brochure had refreshed her memory of the occasion.

Julie had taken a seat by a front window to watch for Kate and had just seen her step out of a new Mercedes sedan. As her luncheon guest approached the hostess stand, Julie waved to catch her attention. Kate saw her and waved back, smiling. A slender blond woman in her fifties, Kate Winslow looked a good ten years younger; she exuded ease and confidence as she made her way to the table. It was easy to see how Bay Street attracted upscale clients.

"Julie, how nice to see you," she said, as they air-kissed. "This is a lovely surprise."

"I hope I'm not taking you away from anything important," said Julie.

"No, no. In fact, your timing couldn't be better! I dropped a pot and cracked the glass on my counter-top stove," she said, laughing. "They're installing a new one later today. I left the whole afternoon open for it, even though they won't be there until after three. You know I only live across the street. I have a townhouse in Venezia."

The waitress came then, and they ordered Cobb salads and another glass of wine for Kate.

"I wanted to tell you how sorry I am about Dianna, Kate. You may not know, but I live next to Lake Eola. I was running out there that morning. I confess that I didn't make the connection between the two of you until recently. I'm so sorry."

As if pulled upward by an invisible string, Kate's inner brows knit together as sadness swiftly changed her expression.

"Thank you. I miss her so much, Julie. I had no idea how much I depended on her, both professionally and personally."

Before she went any further, Julie thought it appropriate to explain her intent.

"I saw Dianna lifted from the swan boat that morning, Kate. It's haunted me ever since. I've offered my services to a private investigator working for the Wielands."

Kate leaned forward with interest.

"Oh, yes. He came to see me. Joe Garrett."

"Right. He's a good friend of mine. Our offices are side-by-side."

The waitress returned with their wine and salads, and Julie resumed when she left.

"So, do you mind if I ask you some questions about Dianna?"

"No, not at all! I don't believe she committed suicide, Julie. I've been utterly dismayed by the newspaper stories.

I'll do anything I can to help you and Joe."

"Great. Well, let's start with business," said Julie. "How long were you two partners?"

"Well…partners…just the last five years. I hired Dianna right out of college when she was only twenty-one. She went to UCF, a Business Admin major. The market was bad and she couldn't find a job, so she got a real estate license and came looking for a broker to place it with."

"You didn't mind hiring someone that young and inexperienced?"

"Not a bit. I prefer to train my agents from scratch so they do things properly. You know the broker always gets left 'holding the bag', so to speak, having to deal with disgruntled customers and lawsuits.

"I've been burned in the past by two *experienced* agents. One misrepresented important facts to a buyer, and another one held back an offer on an apartment building so a friend of his could buy it for less. Sometimes the more they know, the more they think they can get away with."

Julie nodded in agreement.

"Speaking of 'disgruntled customers'…can you tell me about Mike Menello, the contractor Dianna was dealing with, the one who filed a complaint?"

"Oh, *him.* His claim was absolutely baseless," she said. "He was inexperienced and operating on a shoestring. That he was holding Dianna responsible for his loss was incomprehensible! When the police asked me if she had any enemies, Mike Menello was the first person who came to mind…the *only* one, for that matter. I don't know why they haven't taken him into custody."

"He has a good alibi, I understand," said Julie.

"They need to look at him again. I think the man's a natural born liar."

"He does seem to have over-reacted," said Julie in agreement. She took a last sip of her wine. "I think I'm going to have another glass," she said, motioning to the waitress. "Would you like another?"

"Why not?" said Kate. "I'm done for the day."

The waitress brought them two more glasses.

"So, apart from Mike Menello, I take it your clients were happy with Dianna?"

"Oh, yes," said Kate. "We had one fellow, who was *too* happy. He took up her time for two weekends before she realized that he couldn't afford a garage, let alone a house!" She laughed at the recollection. "I kidded her about her pal, Hal… but I was just teasing. Both buyers and sellers loved Dianna for good reason…she was an excellent agent."

"What was she like on a personal level?"

"Well, she *was* ambitious; she liked the good life," said Kate. "Dianna wanted it all."

"By 'all' you mean…?"

"The right husband, children, a place in society," she said. "And a home, preferably in *Isleworth*," she said laughing, "with the rest of the rich and famous."

The wine was clearly having an effect.

"You mentioned children. Dianna wanted children?"

Julie saw immediately that Kate knew. Her eyes welled with tears.

"Yes, she did."

She used her napkin to dab under her eyes.

"I'm sorry, Julie."

"No, Kate. I'm the one who should apologize. I was trying to find out if you already knew about Dianna's pregnancy. The Wielands are adamant about keeping it quiet."

"She just told me two days before," she said. "She was elated, happy."

"Thank you so much for sharing that with me," said Julie. "It's such an important piece of information, Kate. It confirms what I've thought all along. The 'unwanted pregnancy' premise is bull. Dianna was approaching thirty and she wanted a family. She obviously loved kids; she was a volunteer at the YMCA. It all points to one thing: Dianna would have *welcomed* a child."

Julie sat back and asked the most important question of all.

"Did Dianna tell you who the father was?"

"No, she didn't. She was very secretive about the man. She said there were 'some issues,' and that she wanted to tell him first. She was upbeat though, Julie. There was no question about her state of mind."

"What do you mean, her 'state of mind'?"

"Why, she was in love…over the *moon,* in fact…

"Dianna was definitely in love."

16

～

"You have pizza on your chin," said Joe.

"Oops. Where?" said Julie, dabbing in the general area. "Did I get it?"

"Yes, you did," said Joe, amused.

Talking excitedly and eating at the same time was always hazardous for Julie.

They were in Joe's living room, the pizza box set on a huge, square coffee table. Their feet were propped up on either side of it, their plates on their laps. A safe distance behind the pizza box, two fat candles flickered and glowed. It was Julie's little stab at atmosphere, which Joe's apartment sorely lacked. She always thought it looked better in the dark.

"So, I think we need to proceed on the assumption that Dianna was murdered, don't you?"

"Yeah," said Joe, "I do. And there are a few other assumptions we can make. It couldn't have been a robbery; the purse was too easy to get at. And it probably wasn't a random killing because of the odd location and the hour. Someone lured her there."

"Yes. And what about the knife? That's always bothered me. Where would Dianna get a *switchblade*? Women don't use that kind of knife, Joe. The *killer* brought that. Which leads to another question: Why use a knife at all? A knife is messy. A gun is an easier, more reliable way to kill someone."

"It was *personal*," said Joe.

"Bingo," said Julie. "And somehow, she got the knife away from him. Wait a minute, how come *his* prints weren't on it?"

"They probably *were* until she got a hold of it. Think about it. Dianna would have been gripping the knife for all she was worth, Merlin. That would have obliterated any other prints."

Julie sighed.

"Oh, God," she said, stretching her neck back. "I am *so* tired, Joe."

"Not *too* tired, I hope."

He took her empty plate, set it on top of his, and held out his hand.

"Blow out the candles," she said, taking his hand.

Joe picked up a candle and blew it out.

"What else can I do for you?"

———

It was midnight and Joe was snoring softly. Julie hated like hell to get up, but she needed clothes and she needed to tend to Sol. Most of all, she didn't want to run into Luz or Janet if she overslept.

Gathering up her clothes from the bottom of the bed and the floor, she went into the bathroom, careful to close the door as she switched on the light. She dressed quickly, not bothering with a shower. She'd shower and wash her hair in the morning.

Quietly, she left the apartment and descended the staircase past the offices, making sure the front door locked behind her. She got on her scooter, kicked the stand and headed for her condo.

Julie pulled into the garage beneath her building a few minutes later. All the assigned spaces were filled, but it wasn't a problem. She had bought a red VW convertible a year before which was parked in her space. When she pulled the mini-car in, she always left room for the scooter in front of it. She killed the ignition and, still seated, walked the bike between the cars to the front of the VW. Her neighbor's Prius was parked leaving her plenty of space.

God bless Mr. Gladwell. He probably doesn't want me to clip his new car.

Julie never saw her attacker. He came from behind before she got her helmet off. She did manage to press the panic button on her keychain, though.

Twice.

17

"Joe Garrett?" said the woman on the phone.

"Yeah," said Joe, switching on the light, wondering at the unfamiliar voice. Groggy with sleep, he noticed that Julie was gone. He picked up his watch.

It's two; who the hell is calling me?

"Who is this?"

"My name is Megan Sewell, Mr. Garrett. I'm a triage nurse at the ORMC Emergency Room. I'm calling for Julie O'Hara, she gave me your name."

"What? *Julie?"* Joe's stomach lurched as if he'd eaten bad food. "What hospital?"

"Orlando Regional Medical Center, sir. Ms. O'Hara is here in the Emergency Room. She asked me to call you to let you know she was here."

Joe was fully awake now.

"What happened? Is she all right?"

"I can't give you details, sir, but you can come into the Emergency Room and speak to the doctor."

"But what *happened?"*

"She was assaulted, sir. She came in by ambulance. That's all I can tell you," said the nurse. "Do you know where we're located, on Kuhl, off of Orange Ave?"

"Yes, yes, I do. Tell her I'll be right there," he said, hanging up.

Joe pulled on his pants and shirt, and grabbed his wallet and keys off the dresser.

I knew something like this would happen! Why does she have to leave here in the middle of the night! Just so she doesn't run in to Janet or Luz…

Joe was angry with Julie and scared at the same time.

Please, God, let her be all right!

Joe had been in love with Julie for five years, ever since she walked in his door asking about the office space across the foyer. Julie, on the other hand, was icy and barely spoke to him for nearly three years…until her best friend, Marc Solomon, was murdered.

Joe ran down the stairs now and hurried out to the Land Rover. He backed up, then sped down Cypress and turned left on Eola Drive, his mind racing…thinking about Julie.

Their affair had begun during Marc's case and they'd been together since. Joe thought he'd lost her when he proposed a couple months ago; he thought her refusal would spell the end of their relationship. But it hadn't, thank God. Everything was the same.

I'll never pressure her again, God. Please let her be all right…

Joe knew about Julie's husband, knew how traumatized she was by his death. He understood her fear of loss. But Joe had fears, too, and he was afraid of losing her.

The traffic was light. In a matter of minutes, he was parking the Land Rover and running into the Emergency Room. He waited impatiently for a woman to finish her business at the window and move.

"Julie O'Hara. My girlfriend…she's here…a nurse called me. Can I see her?"

A nurse with a clipboard stood behind the woman sitting at the desk. She looked up at him.

"Mr. Garrett?"

"Yes. Can I see Julie O'Hara?"

"Of course. I'm Megan; I called you," she said. "Walk over to the double-doors on your right. I'll let you in."

Everything was beige…the walls, the shiny linoleum floor, the wooden doors that swung open, the wide corridor that stretched before him. It was lined with gurneys, IV's and diagnostic equipment.

Joe followed the heavy set, pony-tailed nurse in her green scrubs, the small squeak of her white sneakers adding to the myriad sounds of the ER, equipment beeping softly, the carefree bantering of two EMT's as they wheeled an old man on a rolling stretcher. He was dimly aware of an intercom voice paging a doctor, but it was the antiseptic smell that unnerved him. It brought back memories of Walter Reed Hospital where he'd gone to visit a friend who was injured by a roadside bomb in Iraq. He'd been unprepared for the horrible damage. He steeled himself now for what might be coming as Nurse Sewell turned, leading him into Julie's room.

Catching his breath, Joe sagged with relief when he finally saw her. Julie was propped up on a gurney, her leg elevated on two pillows and encased in a hard plastic boot. She was conscious and in one piece.

Thank you, God.

A white-coated man with a stethoscope draped around his neck – Indian, perhaps - looked up from his laptop computer, acknowledged them, and continued with his typing.

"Julie…what happened?" said Joe, hugging her.

She sighed and smiled, obviously relieved to see him.

"It was so fast, Joe. I don't know who it was. My head got hit and I fell down. Then he hit me again. It was a bat or something. I pushed the alarm button on my keychain and he ran. That's all I know."

Joe could see that she had been sedated; her eyes were closing. He turned his attention to the doctor and, out of habit, stuck out his hand.

"I'm Joe Garrett," he said, checking out the doctor's name tag. "Dr. Leyva?"

"Yes. Nice to meet you," he said, shaking Joe's hand.

"What's her prognosis, Doctor?" asked Joe.

"It's a fractured fibula, not a major weight-bearing bone," he said, putting up the x-ray. "She doesn't need surgery. The break is high and it's lined-up straight.

You can see it right here," he said, pointing. "And there doesn't appear to be any damage to the tibia.

"That's the good news. The bad news is that she'll be on crutches for three or four weeks, then she's going to need some physical therapy. She has a concussion, so we're going to keep her overnight as a precaution. You'll be able to take her home tomorrow."

"Thank you, Doctor."

"She'll be fine," said Dr. Leyva, as he left the room.

Julie's eyes fluttered open.

"Go to sleep, honey. I'll be here when you wake up."

Joe pulled up a chair and stayed, holding Julie's hand, until her breath was coming slow and easy and she was sound asleep.

Then he drove home…in a cold rage.

This has to be connected with Dianna's murder.

Who the hell is this bastard?

18

⌐∿⌐

"Close the door, please, Luz."

Julie's Latina assistant looked like a worried duenna leaving her young charge alone.

"All right," said Luz. "But you call out if you need me. I can hear you even with the door closed."

Hmm...I'll keep that in mind.

She phoned Joe across the foyer. He picked up right away.

"I swear, Joe, if they don't stop interrupting me, I'm going to have to take this whole file home," said Julie, *sotto voce*. "It's bad enough that Luz is coming in every fifteen minutes to see if I'm alright, but Janet's been in my office twice this morning, too! First she brought me flowers, then *soup*. I can't concentrate with these mother-hens clucking around me."

Joe smiled, chuckling at the picture of Julie, sitting in her office with her left leg propped up, steaming, like her soup.

"Julie says to tell you the soup is *wonderful*, Janet," he said loudly.

Janet, now back at her desk, beamed. "The poor thing," she said. "Tell her I'll bring her some more to take home."

"I'm going to kill you," said Julie on the phone.

———

At quarter to five, Joe joined Julie in her office. Among other things, she'd been going through Dianna Wieland's file piece by piece. As for Joe, he'd been tied up all afternoon testifying in court on another case.

"How did it go?" she asked.

"It was a pain. I spent two hours sitting on a bench outside the courtroom waiting for them to call me. When they did, it was over in fifteen minutes. Plus, I think my guy is toast, anyway."

"Here, let me help you," he said as she lifted her booted leg off the cushions.

"I can manage, thank you," she said, grabbing her crutches.

"Right," said Joe, moving out of her way. "The way you swing those things, you're liable to break *my* leg."

"Don't tempt me."

"Oh, c'mon, lighten up. What do you want for dinner? Italian? Chinese? Steak? I can make steak. Do you still have that patio grill?"

He really is sweet.

"I'd love some steak. Do we have to stop at the store?"

"Nope. I've got two upstairs. I'll be right down."

Since the attack, Joe had been driving Julie back and forth. Her condo building had an elevator, making it more practical than his apartment upstairs. In minutes, he was back with a tote bag of steaks, salad and wine. He grabbed the file on Dianna Wieland, too, and led the way out, holding the doors open for Julie.

When they arrived at her condo, Julie keyed in the code on her new electronic keypad. Joe had installed the new super-bolt door lock, which emitted a shrill alarm if an incorrect code was entered three times. In an excess of caution, he'd also reinforced the French doors around the balcony.

They sat out there now, Julie sipping on some Cabernet, while the steaks cooked.

"I thought of a couple of things today, Joe."

"Okay, shoot."

"First, Sabrina Nolen *was* Mike Menello's alibi. That doesn't make his alibi any less valid, except that she was visibly uncomfortable when I brought up his name."

"I remember that," said Joe. "She sat back and crossed her arms."

"Yes. You know how I've always cautioned that one gesture alone is not as significant as a cluster?"

He nodded.

"Well, two movements we frequently see together are 'interrupt' gestures. Like children in school, we all tend to raise a hand when we want to interrupt, eager to say something. But we don't stick the hand up in the air anymore. We catch ourselves five or six inches up and reach for our earlobe, unconsciously embarrassed."

"I've done that," said Joe smiling. "But Sabrina didn't do that."

"No. She did *exactly the opposite*, in rapid order.

"Sabrina didn't like the question about Mike Menello, so she sat back and crossed her arms. When I pressed her about his 'hard feelings' regarding Dianna, she undid her arms and tugged her earlobe indicating anxiety, *then* her other hand inched up slightly, meaning, 'halt, or stop'. At that point she looked at her watch and we were done.

"That cluster indicates more than a reluctance to talk, Joe. Sabrina is *worried*."

"Do you think she lied for him?"

"I think it's possible."

"Okay. What else?"

"Kate Winslow said that Dianna was '*in love*'. That was Kate's impression just two days before Dianna died at the end of January. I don't think she was in love with Lincoln Tyler. Apparently by her own choice, she hadn't seen him in two months."

"So there's another guy."

"Bingo," said Julie. "People who knew Dianna have described her in a lot of ways. Barry Costello said she was beautiful but not vain, that she was generous, a volunteer with kids. Sabrina Nolen said she was fun to be with. They've talked about Dianna's *other* faces, too. Kate Winslow said she was ambitious and somewhat secretive. Evelyn Hoag said she tended to be naïve.

"One thing's for sure, though; Dianna made an indelible impression on people she interacted with. At some level, they miss her. They all wanted to talk about her.

"All, except for one person: *Lee Porter.*

"Looking back on it, I realize that Porter said virtually *nothing* about Dianna. When I spoke with him, I noticed right away that he was reluctant to talk to me, but I presumed it was about the complaint against Bay Street Realty. Seasoned attorney that he is, he took full advantage of my preoccupation with that complaint. By focusing my attention on Mike Menello, Lee Porter took *himself* completely off my radar."

"And Porter is *married*," said Joe.

"Right. Dianna told Kate there were some 'issues'. Her baby's father being married to someone else would certainly qualify as an '*issue*'. It would also be a naïve and hopeful way to describe the situation, which fits with Evelyn Hoag's description of Dianna believing 'in happy endings'."

"So you think Evelyn Hoag knew about it."

"If it *was* Lee Porter, she would have had to. Dianna couldn't contact Porter at his home. Their communication would have gone through the office. Plus Evelyn and Dianna were 'close friends'. And how did that friendship come about? Maybe because Evelyn was a *confidante*, is my guess. As Porter's secretary, she was probably an unwilling facilitator for the two of them."

"So, now what? We can't confront Lee Porter with guesses."

"No. Our only shot is Evelyn."

19

Evelyn Hoag arrived at Julie's condo at half-past five the next evening. Thanks to Joe's hurried trip to the market, Julie had managed to prepare a platter of French bread, smoked turkey, sliced apples and Brie. The two women sat on the balcony, Julie with her back to the lake and her booted leg propped on a chair. Sol, always comfortable with women, was lying near Evelyn who was relaxing and enjoying the view. In between sips of Chardonnay, she absently stroked his back.

"I'd already made up my mind to contact you, Julie. I owe that much to Dianna."

"Thanks for coming here," said Julie. "I haven't tried to navigate a restaurant yet with these crutches."

Prior to Evelyn's arrival, Julie had prepared for the questions she would ask about Lee Porter. When she opened the door, the first thing Evelyn asked about was the boot, for which Julie was completely *un*prepared. Not wanting to alarm her or divert their conversation, Julie had quickly come up with a plausible story. "A running injury," she'd said. "I snapped my fibula. I won't be able to run again for at least three months." Not until that moment had Julie realized just how much she missed her morning run around the lake.

As planned, Julie proceeded with the assumptive tactic she'd used on the phone.

"So when did their affair start, Evelyn?"

"About two years ago. Amazing, isn't it? Keeping something like that a secret here in Orlando. But they met outside of town and went to secluded inns in out-of-the-way places, like Mt. Dora and Lake Helen." Her face suddenly contorted with pain. "Oh," she said, leaning forward. Her face was in her hands now, her dark hair like a veil closing from the sides.

"What is it?" asked Julie, alarmed.

"Lake Helen. They went there first. I was remembering what she told me about the fortune teller…"

20

March 14, 2008

"I've never been to Lake Helen," said Dianna. "Where is it?"

"It's about an hour north on I-4, before you get to Daytona. Can you leave now? We can meet at the Amtrak station in Sanford. I'll leave my car there and we'll go the rest of the way in yours, if that's all right."

"That's fine, Lee. It's more than fine, it's wonderful!"

Dianna was elated as she selected just the right lingerie. In less than ten minutes she had gathered her things and was in her Lexus, headed northeast on I-4. She had been yearning for this tryst with Lee for more than a year. For all that time they had been attracted to each other, drawn inexorably closer with each mutual business meeting.

In the beginning, she had rebuked herself on moral grounds.

He's married. He's forty-three.

But their eyes continued to hold each other a little longer on each occasion and it became increasingly difficult to concentrate on the day's business. Sitting next to Lee at a conference table full of others was tantalizing…the stuff of guilty, x-rated dreams.

Finally, he had asked her to lunch. Briefcases in tow, they took a table in a Winter Park restaurant, all alone in a crowd. More lunches and shared confidences followed, and Dianna's moral paradigm shifted.

He doesn't love Sylvia. They have no children. Our ages don't really matter.

Dianna was a romantic, but she was also an intelligent woman who had moved from rationalization to analysis. Despite the evening commuter traffic between Orlando and Sanford, the miles flew by as she thought about the two of them.

Lee Porter was a father figure, of that she had no doubt.

It wasn't that Dianna's dominating father didn't love her. She knew that he did, but only as an extension of himself. As an adult, Dianna had come to accept this shortcoming. But it was too late to repair damage already done.

As a toddler, she'd learned to skate to please her father. As she grew older and won skating awards, her Dad, an ex-hockey player, had basked in reflected glory. They were inseparable and happy. Unfortunately, when Dianna was fifteen, she could no longer deny the true framework of their relationship. She was telling her father about a friend who worked as a counselor at a summer camp, going on about the kids and the things they did, when she realized that he was looking at her with blatant disinterest. It was hardly the first time, just the first time she acknowledged it. Her father had no interest in her personal musings because they did not involve him. She loved him for himself, and he loved her for *himself*. It was all about *him*. The crushing truth of it came too suddenly, at a vulnerable age. It blew their once-close relationship apart.

Lee was obviously a father figure who plugged the gaping holes in that original, devastated landscape. Dianna knew it and embraced it.

Lee loved her for herself.

He was leaning against his Toyota Highlander when she pulled into the parking lot. Though dressed in jeans and a polo shirt, there was still a Cary Grant elegance about him.

He tossed his tennis duffle-bag into the back seat. "Hi," he said.

Dianna thought he was the handsomest man she'd ever seen.

"You drive," she said. "You know where we're headed."

A small voice said, *where are we headed, Lee?* But Dianna pushed it away.

———

They drove through gently rolling hills into Lake Helen near the St. Johns River. Country lanes took them past turn of the century homes and churches. Lee pulled to a stop at a secluded inn:

The Ann Stevens House, 1895.

A winding brick walk took them to their room in the Carriage House, a later addition, more private than the main house. It had all the bells and whistles: a private verandah, a Jacuzzi and a fireplace. They couldn't have cared less…their only interest was the big bed in the middle.

As soon as the door closed behind them, Lee's arm encircled Dianna's waist, drawing her close. They kissed deeply, passionately. Her hands moved over his back and shoulders, delighting in the hard strength of him. She was eager, so eager to feel the length of his body against her bare skin. She grabbed the bottom of her jersey and pulled it up and off. She stepped out of her linen Capri pants.

Lee audibly sucked in his breath. Dianna's breasts were softly mounding over the top of a lacy, low-cut brassiere. Another patch of lace barely covered the shaved hair between her legs.

His instantaneous reaction was gratifying and exciting. Then her brassiere was off and his hands were on her breasts, squeezing them, raising her nipples. His mouth was tugging on her breast and his hand was moving inside her. Dianna couldn't take another moment.

"Now, Lee, now," she gasped, backing up to the bed.

Fortunately, Sherlock's Pub, right in the Carriage House, was still open. Neither of them had eaten since breakfast. Having satisfied their desire for one another, they were now devouring cheeseburgers with only slightly less gusto.

They were surrounded by images of Sherlock Holmes and his friend, Watson.

"Did you know Sir Arthur Conan Doyle was a spiritualist?" asked Lee.

"No. You mean as a religion?"

"Well, I don't know about that," said Lee. "He was a lapsed Catholic, I think. But he was also a believer in clairvoyance. He attended séances and things like that."

"How odd, I never knew that."

"Not only that, we're right next to Cassadaga."

"Ohmigod, the fortune-tellers! I've never had my fortune told. Can we go there in the morning before we go home?"

"I think they prefer to be called 'psychics'," said Lee, laughing. "But, yes. That was the idea; I thought you might enjoy it."

"Have you gone before?" she asked.

"Yes. Years ago. A woman named Sophie. She was surprisingly accurate."

―――

Dianna felt a vague disappointment. The village of Cassadaga was more quaint than mystical. Ordinary houses were interspersed with new-age gift shops and art galleries. Lee was driving around the small area, losing hope about finding his psychic, Sophie, of twenty years past.

"Has it changed that much?" asked Dianna.

"No, not much. It's funny. I remember being in her kitchen, but I can't remember which house it was. None of these look familiar."

They got out of the car in front of a building with a prominent sign:

Universal Centre.

Inside, Dianna browsed through a rack of brochures reading about "ethereal vibrations" and "energy hot spots" while listening to Lee as he spoke to a woman.

"Sophie? You must mean Reverend Sophie Tindall. She's one of the oldest psychics in our organization."

"Is she still doing readings?"

"Oh, yes. Not as many as before, but I can assure you she's more sensitive than ever."

"Where is her house?" asked Lee.

The woman gave him a street map, pointing out the house.

"Twenty-nine Acacia Lane," she said.

Lee thanked her and they headed back to the car.

"No wonder I couldn't find the house. It's two blocks behind here."

The bungalow fit right into the landscape. Vines crept up on the wood-shingled roof and a spreading sweet acacia threatened to engulf one end of the wide, sagging porch. The house sat on cinder blocks, exactly as Lee had described it. Someone had recently taken a stab at maintenance and repainted all the trim white.

Dianna and Lee climbed the stairs and knocked on the front door, which sported a small, diamond-shaped window. The edge of a curtain was pulled back, and the door opened.

"Hello. Are you looking for a reading?" said a tiny woman, her gray hair pulled back in a bun. Her eyes were a very clear blue, except for a noticeable cataract on the left.

"Yes," said Lee. "You wouldn't remember me, Sophie; I was here many years ago."

"Oh, yes. Of course, of course," she said, ushering them in.

Dianna didn't believe for a moment that she remembered Lee.

"I brought my friend for a reading," said Lee, "if you have the time."

"Of course," she said. "You can wait out here with Edward."

Dianna smiled as the woman directed Lee to an old upholstered swivel chair next to its twin, currently occupied by a snoring old man.

Lee reluctantly sat, as Sophie led Dianna into the kitchen and closed the door behind them.

"Sit, my dear," she said, taking her own seat at a small oak table. "Tell me about yourself."

Tell you about myself? I thought you were supposed to tell me.

Seeing the expression on Dianna's face, the woman said, "Just generally. What is your first name? Do you live in Florida? Are you married?"

"I'm sorry. My name is Dianna, and I do live in Florida. I'm not married."

"All right, Dianna," said Sophie, gently. "Let me hold your hands."

Dianna held out her hands and Sophie took them, closing her eyes.

The woman said nothing. Dianna's skepticism grew steadily as the cypress clock on the wall loudly ticked off the seconds, then the minutes. Still, feeling slightly foolish, she waited.

Suddenly, Sophie opened her eyes and spoke.

"He will cover you with his feathers. Under his wings you will find refuge."

Dianna waited for her to continue, but the woman had given her hands a squeeze and let go.

"Can I ask you questions?" said Dianna. "Do you see marriage in my future?"

"I'm sorry, my dear, I'm afraid that's all I can tell you. It's a message from God. You'll have to figure out how it fits into your life."

"So, are you going to tell me what she said?"

Dianna told him.

"That's it?" Lee said.

"That's it. I'm not sure if it's a message from God or a fortune cookie."

They both laughed…

21

It was a Bible verse, Julie recalled, out of context…and yet…wings, feathers, refuge.

Had Dianna found refuge in the swan boat?

"Dianna didn't kill herself. I just don't believe it," said Evelyn, getting up. She stood at the balcony railing looking out at the lake. "I think somebody attacked her. Maybe she got into that swan boat to get away."

"Maybe she did," said Julie.

"Evelyn…did you know that Dianna was seeing another man besides Lee?"

"Yes, Linc Tyler…her 'cowboy'. She told me about him."

"I don't understand," said Julie. "If Dianna was so in love with Lee, how did she get involved with Lincoln Tyler?"

"I think it was to get back at Lee. From the way Sylvia Porter was calling the office, I think she suspected that Lee was cheating on her. She began showing up for lunch unannounced, telling him at the

114

last moment about dinners they had to attend. Lee was canceling plans with Dianna – actually, I was – left and right.

"Dianna was furious. They had a huge fight. She told him she didn't want to see him anymore. I supported her completely. Dianna didn't need to play second fiddle; she could have had anybody."

"Did Lee know about Lincoln?"

"He thought Dianna was seeing someone. He asked me all kinds of questions. I didn't tell him anything. I would never have betrayed her confidence in me."

She sat at the table again. Tears were running down her face. She grabbed a napkin and dabbed around her eyes, her cheeks. Sol looked up at her, as if sensing her distress…and Julie waited, respecting her grief.

"So Dianna stopped seeing him?"

"Yes. For a few months. He left her messages, sent her flowers. He repeatedly asked, 'Did Dianna call?' He was crazy without her. I shouldn't have told her, but I did…and she started to see him again."

"Evelyn…you said they only broke up for 'a few months'…so…Dianna was seeing both men at the same time?"

"Yes. She told me Linc Tyler wanted to marry her. I believe she was considering it for a while…until Lee told her he was going to leave Sylvia. Until he leased the condo…"

"What condo?"

Evelyn looked away, hesitating.

She doesn't want to tell me...feels like she has to...to clear her conscience.

"The one Downtown here, on Franklin Street."

"Franklin?"

"Yes. Across the lake."

22

~

November 26, 2009

Sylvia Brandt-Porter deftly twisted her husband's tie into a perfect bow.

"Really, Lee, why do you insist on wearing tennis cufflinks to a formal dinner?"

He sighed and turned away, not bothering to answer her.

Because Dianna gave them to me.

It was so much harder to tolerate Sylvia now. Lee didn't even *like* her anymore.

When did that happen? Was it year two, or three?

Whichever it was, it was shortly after his law partner, James Brandt, walked her down the aisle. Lee remembered being happy on that day, glancing at Sylvia beneath her veil, soft blonde waves framing her face. Her elegant profile had reminded him of a delicately carved cameo. Things were good then. Sylvia was fun to be with, a friend with benefits. Lee had honestly expected their friendship to grow into love.

117

Right. It was our first anniversary. What a joke.

Inspired by their wedding day, Lee had known what Sylvia's first anniversary gift would be. He ordered a hand-carved Sardonyx shell cameo from Italy. He was so excited when it arrived. He thought it was beautiful, high relief set in gold, on a fine gold chain. He'd kept it in the office where she wouldn't find it, and presented it to her on their anniversary over dinner at Le Coq Au Vin. He held her hand and explained why he'd chosen a cameo for her.

Sylvia was "touched"; it was a "wonderful gift".

Lee couldn't remember her ever wearing it…not even once.

Screw you. I'm wearing my tennis cufflinks.

———

Dianna walked into her townhouse and hit the button on her answering machine.

"Received December first at ten-forty-seven-a-m," said the recorded voice. And then it was Lee: *"I've leased a condo, Dianna. I've already moved some of my things. I'm leaving her right after the holidays. Please, please, call me back. I love you."*

He was leaving her! She played the message again. He was moving!

Overcome with emotion, Dianna walked around in a tight circle, tears running down her face, her hands clasped at her chin as if in thankful prayer. She picked up the phone and began to key in the familiar number, then quickly hung it up.

What should I say? I shouldn't be so easy. It's not like he's already moved! Evelyn said he would never *leave Sylvia. What if she's right? It makes sense, though, to wait until after the holidays. It would be cruel to leave before then. I should at least see him.*

She punched in the number.

"Porter and Brandt."

"Hi, Evelyn. Is Lee there?"

"Hello, Dianna," she said, whispering into the phone. *"I thought you might call. Are you sure you want to do this?"*

It was at times like this that Dianna got angry with Evelyn.

"Yes, Evelyn, I'm sure. Please put me through."

In a moment, Lee was on the line.

"Dianna?"

"Hello, Lee."

"Oh, God. I'm so glad to hear your voice. I've missed you so much. When can I see you?"

"You're the one who has trouble getting away," said Dianna.

"Not for long, that's what I want to talk to you about. Can you meet me tonight?"

"All right. Where?"

"Downtown. Let's meet at seven, Kres Chophouse. I'll take you to see the condo after dinner. I'd ask you to stay, but I don't have a bed yet," he said laughing.

Dianna smiled and then steeled herself. She would not be that easy.

———

"Well, how do you like it?" said Lee, as he went about lighting candles that reflected on the dark, polished granite of the kitchen bar and a lonely square glass coffee table in the living room. He flicked on the Bose CD player and soft, romantic music floated through the sparsely furnished apartment. A bottle of wine nestled in a silver bucket of ice alongside two fine-stemmed glasses.

Dianna was fully aware of what he was doing.

"It's a nice Downtown location. It will probably be convenient for you."

"For *us*," he said, taking her in his arms.

All high-minded thoughts flew away as his hands moved over her body.

In the empty living room, with new carpet for a bed, Dianna dissolved in a pool of pleasure without a drop of pride.

23

"So Porter already went to the cops?" asked Joe.

They were in Joe's Land Rover headed to Lee and Sylvia Porter's house in Winter Park.

"Yes. Evelyn told him she couldn't keep the condo secret any longer, even if it meant losing her job. She knew Lee and Dianna were supposed to meet at the condo that night. Dianna had called the office and left a confirming message for him with Evelyn.

"Lee swore up and down that he changed his mind and *didn't* meet Dianna, that he was with Sylvia all night, but Evelyn wasn't sure she believed him. She told him she wouldn't go to the police, but she was going to talk to me about it. You have to give her credit; that took a lot of guts.

"I don't know, maybe it was weighing on him, too, Joe. She didn't lose her job, after all. He said he understood and asked her to stay. He just asked her to give him time to volunteer his information to the police."

"And he agreed to meet with us...*with* his wife," said Joe. "So, he must have come clean with her, too."

"Well, she's his alibi," said Julie. "This will be an interesting meeting."

They were in an old established neighborhood on the shores of Lake Maitland. Joe pointed out the Winter Park Racquet Club.

"I heard Brandt was one of the charter members," he said.

Julie was looking for Moss Drive and didn't hear him.

"Who was?"

"James Brandt, Porter's partner."

"There's Moss Drive," said Julie.

Number four-eighty-seven was huge, with pillars and arches and a barrel-tile roof. It was all one floor, but sprawling. Like most homes on the old lakefront street, the original house was long gone. Julie thought that the Porters must have torn down two old houses to build this one with its attached three-car garage. They pulled into the bricked circular driveway, got out and rang the bell. Julie half expected a butler to answer, but it was Lee Porter.

"Hi, Joe. Julie," he said somberly. "Come in, please."

They stepped into a wide, marble-floored room which overlooked a pool and the lake. The room was split into two areas, left and right, by two square tray ceilings bordered with dark wood beams. Matching wrought iron chandeliers hung from each, centered above two identical floral rugs. The left square was a dining area, and the right a living room with a green velvet sofa and floral chairs. On the far right sat a baby grand piano.

Sylvia Porter sat in the living room in front of a fringed ottoman that held a large tray and a tea service. She wore a single strand of pearls over a pale green sweater and skirt. There wasn't a blonde hair out of place in her French twist. She held a cup of tea and didn't bother to get up.

Lee directed them to the sofa and took a chair on their left. Sylvia was on their right. A middle chair, directly in front of them sat empty.

Great...a tennis match.

"Sylvia, you remember Julie O'Hara, and this is Joe Garrett."

He turned to Julie and Joe.

"My wife, Sylvia."

"How do you do," she said with a quick smile that involved no other part of her face.

"Would you like some tea?" said Lee.

Julie declined and was glad that Joe did, too. This was going to be uncomfortable.

"First," said Lee, "I want to apologize, Julie. I should have been more forthcoming when you came to my office. I wasn't," he said, glancing at Sylvia, "for a very obvious reason."

"We understand," said Joe.

Personally, Julie thought Lee was a cliché, regardless of his misery.

"Would you tell us what you told the police?" asked Julie.

"I told them about our affair and about leasing the condominium by the lake. I told them that she stayed there that night, that I was planning to join her but I never went there. Sylvia and I were at a late dinner party, and then we came home here together."

Lee's forearms were resting on the arms of his chair. He unconsciously turned his palms slightly upward as he spoke but not in an exaggerated manner.

He's relaxed, blinking at a normal rate. The pitch of his voice is normal. He got right to the point, no irrelevant information. His feet and legs are still. His body language is congruent. He's telling the truth...but a censored version...because of Sylvia?

Julie turned to Sylvia, who was a statue with a teacup on her knee.

"So the two of you were together all night?"

If looks could kill, I would be dead right now.

"Yes," said Sylvia, placing her cup on the ottoman tray. "For a change, Lee was with me the entire night." She stood up, straightening her skirt. "Now that I've told the police and the two of you, I think I'll leave. Unless there's something else you need *me* for? Lee?"

Her tone was icy, but there was no mistaking the truthfulness of her statement.

"No. Thank you, Sylvia," said Lee.

Sylvia walked out of the room.

"Well," said Lee, "that's it. I couldn't get away. I don't know what else to tell you."

NOW you're lying. Your hand just went to your face, you shifted in the chair. I can see the whites on the bottom of your eyes. You're lying.

"Excuse me for being blunt, Lee, but there is something else. Dianna wasn't waiting in a bar. Evidently, she spent the *whole night* in your condo, so it didn't matter if you were late. Exactly *why* didn't you meet her?"

His first phone call to Dianna was at ten o'clock.

"I can't believe it. We're just sitting down to dinner! I thought they'd never get past the damn cocktails. I'm calling from the bathroom. I'm sorry, honey, I'm going to be late."

"Don't worry, Lee. It's alright. I've got clothes here and everything I need."

"Okay. Maybe another hour…I'll be there soon."

He made the second phone call from his car at quarter to twelve. She was sleeping. She sounded a little groggy. Maybe she had some wine?

"Sorry to wake you, honey. I'm almost there."

"Good. I was dreaming. I have good news, Lee," she said, sleepily. "I'm pregnant. I love you so much. See you soon."

Lee pulled off the road. He sat there for a few minutes. Then he did a u-turn and headed for Winter Park.

"So that stopped you from going there?" said Joe, shocked and not a little disgusted.

Lee turned and looked right at him.

"Yes, it did. I had a vasectomy four years ago."

24

"Well that was fun," said Joe, heading back to the office.

"At least we know why Dianna was at Lake Eola," said Julie.

"Which means it was a crime of opportunity or she was followed," said Joe.

"Right. But I don't think it was random. We already decided that, remember? No robbery, no sexual assault."

"Yeah, but this changes things, Merlin. We know that the killer *didn't* lure her there. The odds are that Dianna woke up and realized Lee wasn't coming, so she headed to her car. That makes *other* scenarios more likely. It *could* have been a mugging gone wrong, someone drunk or strung out on drugs. That would fit with a switchblade, too; they don't usually have guns.

"And I know you don't want to hear this, Julie, but it also strengthens the current theory. Dianna may have realized that Lee didn't come because of the baby. What would that have done to her romantic dreams of a 'happy ending?' Maybe she just wanted an *ending*."

Julie was subdued for the rest of the drive, even after they split up and she returned to her own office. Joe's logic was unassailable, but she still didn't buy the suicide angle. From all that she knew of the woman, Julie felt that Dianna's reaction to being stood-up would have been *anger*, not despair. Dianna might have been an optimist, but she wasn't fragile.

Hell, didn't she manage to grab the knife from an attacker?

Julie knew in her heart that she *did*. Dianna certainly wasn't walking around with a switchblade in a little Louis Vuitton bag…a zipped bag, at that. Who would bother re-zipping a purse after they slit their wrist?

There's no way she killed herself.

Okay, that's settled.

Could it have been a crime of opportunity, though? Was Dianna simply in the wrong place at the wrong time?

Julie reluctantly had to admit the possibility. Still, there was an awful lot of passion swirling around Dianna Wieland. She was simultaneously involved with two men, one of them married, with the further complication of a pregnancy. That was a volatile situation. And she had a bitter enemy in Mike Menello.

The phone on her desk rang, startling her.

"This is Merlin," she said.

"*Julie, you'd better come over,*" said Joe. "*Betty Wieland's on her way. She said she has something she needs to show us.*"

25

Promptly at half-past one, Betty Wieland walked into Joe's office carrying a shoebox. She greeted Julie and Joe, and looked nervously toward Janet Hawkins, seated at her desk.

It wasn't the first time a client did that, and Janet immediately pulled her purse from a drawer and stood.

"Do you mind if I go to lunch now, Boss?"

"No. Go ahead, take your time," said Joe.

As Janet ducked out the door, Joe pulled up a third chair for Betty and offered her some coffee. She declined and sat there clutching the battered shoebox on her lap, her body on the edge of the chair, angled toward the door as if reconsidering her decision to come.

"Frank can't know I'm here. I told him I had a dental appointment. But you said you wanted to know my Dianna better, to understand her life. And when I found this box…"

Julie put her hand on top of Betty's hand.

"We're glad you came, Betty. It was the right thing to do."

She looked at Julie gratefully. Sitting back, she set the box on the desk.

There was an uncomfortable silence.

Joe knew better than to touch the box in front of him.

"What did you want to tell us, Betty?"

"I don't know where to begin."

Julie looked at the old, beat-up Thom McAn shoebox.

"Start in Massachusetts, Betty," she said gently.

———

"Dianna was in the ninth grade when she began to turn against us," said Betty. "I shouldn't really put it that way, I suppose. She was fifteen. All teenagers are embarrassed by their parents at that age, aren't they? But we'd always been so close, you see.

"Our lives circled around her. I never worked. I wanted to be there for her when she came home from school. That was my job…to help Dianna with her homework, to do her clothes, to drive her to the shopping mall or to a friend's house. And Frank, he became like her coach with the skating, taking her everywhere.

"I should explain," she said, looking at Julie and Joe.

"Frank played hockey when he was young, until he broke his leg. He was a big Bruins fan. Bobby Orr was his idol. I think he wanted to *be* Bobby Orr. Anyway, we took Dianna skating on Horn Pond when she was just a little girl. Frank made such a big deal out of everything she did on the ice! Well, you can figure out the rest. Dianna loved her Daddy and wanted to please him. I thought it was sad, in a way. They never talked about anything else but skating. It was all Frank was really interested in."

Betty stopped and sighed.

"My Dianna was a pretty child, but by the time she was fifteen she was *beautiful*. People don't think of that as a burden, but when it comes to teenagers, they're wrong. She got too much attention, too quickly. Her skating and her looks opened doors for her. Girls wanted to be like her, and *boys*…well, our phone rang off the hook.

"Dianna began to hang around with kids who were the elite crowd in her school. They came from well-off families. And that became a problem because we *weren't*, you see. It wasn't that Dianna was ashamed of us, really. She was just impressed by their affluence. This one had designer clothes, and that one got a convertible for graduation, and so-and-so had a pool and a tennis court.

"We did the best we could with clothes and things, but the rest was out of our league.

"Frank was irked by her '*attitude*'. He became stricter and more demanding. He forbade her to see this friend and that friend. And Dianna pushed back in *every* way she could. She wouldn't clean her room or get up for church. She was deliberately late coming home when she went out. Finally, she quit skating. That was the last straw for my husband.

"I tried to keep the peace. I told him to choose his battles, not to fight with Dianna over unimportant things like going to church or keeping a spotless room.

If she wanted to stop skating, that was up to *her*. I felt our focus should be on her safety and her school work.

"But, of course, he wouldn't listen to me.

"Frank had always had an iron grip on Dianna, primarily through her skating, and he was determined to keep her under his thumb, one way or another. He grounded her indefinitely, allowed her out only for school. He didn't lock her in her room, but he might as well have, because that was her only refuge. Eventually, she snuck out to see some of her friends. Frank called the parents of each and every one of them. He told them that Dianna wasn't allowed to see their son or daughter anymore, that they were a 'bad influence' on his child.

"As you can imagine, the parents he contacted were insulted. They made absolutely *sure* that their kids stayed away from her. In a matter of months, Dianna was completely isolated. She was like a princess locked in a tower. She couldn't have been more vulnerable."

She paused and laid her hand on the shoebox for just a moment.

Joe's attention was riveted on the box, but Julie studied Betty.

Unconsciously, Betty pulled back her hand, tucking her hair behind her ear.

Distraction. This is so hard for her to talk about.

"It wasn't really her fault," she said softly.

"What wasn't her fault, Betty?" asked Julie gently.

"What happened with Hoyt."

26

Massachusetts, 1996

She'd left her books at school. What was the point of studying? There was no point to anything anymore. Her life was *ruined*.

Dianna trudged up the long hill toward her house.

It was his fault. He never loved *her*; he loved being the father of a skating champion. She was nothing to him but an extension of himself. She always knew it, deep down. When did he ever ask her what *she* thought, or how *she* felt about anything?

She hated skating! She hated *him*.

Totally absorbed in her misery, Dianna had stopped caring about a lot of things. No longer did she spend time straightening her long dark hair or choosing just the right preppy outfit. She'd been completely dropped by her fair-weather friends, so what was the point?

Alicia Wells was the only friend Dianna had left. A skating buddy who lived around the corner, she was the only person allowed to visit. Closeted in Dianna's bedroom, Alicia would whisper the latest gossip. Although Dianna was grateful to have at least *one* friend, the news of all that was going on only served to make her feel more excluded and angry.

To hell with them! she thought.

Fuming, she strode on up the hill, never noticing the truck slowing down beside her.

"Hi!"

She whipped her head around and glared at the driver.

It was Hoyt Geller from North Street Farm.

A moment or two passed before he spoke.

"Want a ride?"

———

As usual Hoyt had trouble breathing when he looked at Dianna.

His first glimpse of her was two years prior when her family came to skate.

The Geller's farm on North Street was principally apple orchards, but they also had horse trails and hayrides. In the winter, two shallow ponds on their property froze solid and the family cleared them for skating.

Hoyt was sixteen then. He had been manning a hut between the "twins", as they called the two ponds, selling coffee and cocoa to the skaters. Dianna came in, her head down, pulling off her gloves, fumbling in her fur-trimmed jacket for change. When she raised her head, Hoyt literally stopped breathing.

Her face was perfectly shaped, framed by dark tresses of hair spilling out of the fur-trimmed hood. Incredible blue-green eyes fringed with long, dark lashes looked up at him. She stood up straight, almost as tall as he. Her creamy skin was flushed by the cold. She was smiling at him, perfect white teeth and full, pink lips.

Hoyt had wanted desperately to ask her out. He approached a friend of his, to find out her name. The boy laughed at him.

"Are you crazy, man? She's only thirteen!"

Hoyt was dumbfounded. He watched Dianna doing pirouettes and axels on the pond. He had never seen anything so beautiful in his life.

Except for now, at this moment, as she spun around to stare into his truck.

This was a different Dianna, as exotic and enticing as a gypsy. Her hair was wild and full and her eyes were flashing with intensity. They were green today, like the jersey that clung to her breasts. It took him a couple moments to find his voice.

"Want a ride?"

———

Why not? thought Dianna, as she climbed in next to Hoyt.

"Where are you headed?" asked Hoyt.

"Home. You can let me off at the top of the hill, at the corner."

They rode for a few moments in silence.

"Want to go for a Smoothie?" blurted Hoyt, blushing for some reason.

Dianna glanced at him, for the first time realizing how good looking he was. What was her rush? It was only three o'clock; her father wouldn't be home until after five.

"Sure."

Conversation was easy between them and Dianna found Hoyt more and more attractive. He looked different than the boys at school, more mature. And he was funny! He did impressions and made her laugh. They talked on and on like old friends, and the time flew by.

Dianna stole a glance at her watch; it was half-past four! She had to get home!

"I have to go," she said. "I have to get home before my father." Seeing Hoyt's puzzled expression, she told him what was going on at home.

"So you can't go out?"

Suddenly, she realized that Hoyt wanted to see her again, like on a *date*. And just as quickly, Dianna knew she wanted the same thing.

"If I wait until they're asleep, I can sneak out for a little while."

"What about tonight?"

"It would be late," she said, "after eleven."

"That's okay," said Hoyt. "I'll wait for you at the corner."

"Where have you been?" said her mother. "Thank heavens you got home before your father, Dianna! Go up and change your clothes. I'll call you when dinner's ready."

Dianna could barely wait for the time to go by. Dinner was interminable, her father's presence unbearable. He no longer spoke to her. He communicated by *looks*.

When the meal was over, he gave her a look that said, "Get up and help your mother." When the dishes were done and she walked into the living room, his look said, "What are you doing in here? Go to your room." That was something she was happy enough to do tonight. She wished they would go to *theirs*.

Eventually it was silent in the house and safe to leave. She couldn't go out the front or the back door. When Frank caught her before, he'd locked her out all night in the freezing cold. Dianna wasn't going to chance *that* again.

Her bedroom was on the second floor of their modest colonial-style home. The side window was just above a small porch roof. The porch had a door in the rear, which gave the family access to a brick outdoor grill. The grill was cleverly built on the outside of the living-room's fireplace, matching the brick chimney.

It was also nicely stepped…for climbing.

———

Dianna had been meeting Hoyt once or twice a week for over a month. At first, Hoyt just drove and they talked, but that had evolved into parking and fooling around. Now he got right to it, pulling the truck in behind the maintenance shed at the golf course near her house. He slid over and pulled her into his arms as soon as he cut the ignition.

His lips felt so soft and moist as they moved from her mouth to her neck. His hand slipped inside her cotton brassiere and cupped her breast, brushing her nipple. Dianna felt like she was melting away, falling, falling. His hand massaged between her legs and she felt a fluttering inside like never before, and then he was pulling the elastic aside…

"No, no. Stop, Hoyt. I can't."

"I love you, Dianna. I want you."

They were magic words to her, almost irresistible. Almost.

———

Dianna told Alicia everything.

"Oh my God, Dianna, he's so *hot*!"

"I know. It's so hard to stop."

"That's funny," said Alicia, giggling.

"What's funny?"

"You said 'It's so *hard*'. Did you see it?"

Dianna put her finger to her lips. "*No!* Be quiet. My mother is upstairs," she mouthed.

"I told Chrissy and Melissa. They are *so* jealous," whispered Alicia. "They think Hoyt is *so* handsome.

When are you seeing him again?"

"Tonight. But we have to stop; I'm afraid I'm going to get caught. My father will kill me."

"Everyone thinks you and Hoyt should just run away and get married," whispered Alicia. "*Lots* of people find the right guy and get married when they're young, you know."

Something about their conversation was very satisfying to Dianna. *She had friends again; friends who were on her side.*

"How would we do it?"

"You could go to New Hampshire, to a Justice of the Peace. You don't even need blood tests in New Hampshire, you just have to go up and apply for a marriage license a month or so ahead of time."

"How do you know that?"

"I went on my mother's computer and looked it up," said Alicia, smugly.

"How old do you have to be?"

"Eighteen. But it's easy enough to get a fake driver's license. *Everybody* gets them so they can drink. And Hoyt's already eighteen."

That night Dianna dreamt about marrying Hoyt, about escaping her father.

———

"Please, please," begged Hoyt as if in a trance, pressing Dianna's hand against the bulge between his legs. He started to pull the zipper down.

"No, don't, Hoyt," said Dianna, afraid and pulling away.

"Oh, I can't stand this!" He jumped out of the truck and began pacing back and forth, running his hands through his hair. After a while, he calmed down and climbed back in.

"I'm sorry," said Dianna, tears running down her face. "I just don't feel right about it. I mean here, like this."

He took her face in his hands and kissed her tenderly.

"It's okay. I shouldn't have lost it like that. It's just that I love you so much."

She kissed him back and then looked in his eyes.

"Do you want to marry me, Hoyt?"

Dianna's mother sighed in frustration.

"Frank, it's just five or six girls, *a pajama party*, for heaven's sake. Let her go."

"Did you talk to Alicia's mother?" he said. "I don't trust divorced women."

"Of course I did. Jane Wells is a good woman; Dianna will be fine with her."

"All right. But I want her home first thing in the morning."

"Frank, tomorrow is Saturday. There's no school."

"I don't care. You tell Dianna I want her home, in her room by ten, you hear me?"

The elopement of the star-crossed lovers was planned with great secrecy and enthusiasm.

Alicia Wells knew that her mother, as usual, would be proof reading in her home office that night. Once Jane Wells had seen to it that the girls were encamped in the basement playroom with their pizza and games, she would stay upstairs and give them their privacy.

Hoyt would be waiting for Dianna at seven o'clock, sharp. The plan was for them to drive to New Hampshire, get married and spend their "honeymoon night" in a motel. Hoyt would return Dianna to Alicia's house just before dawn. In a week or so they would inform their parents of the *fait accompli*. Everyone would have to accept the fact that they were married. Then Hoyt and Dianna would get a small apartment. All the girls thought it was just *so* romantic!

None of them had a clue about the disaster they had set in motion.

———

It was far from the way Dianna had imagined her wedding day would be. They had barely made it in time. The "Justice of the Peace" was about to shut off his porch light and go to bed when Hoyt and Dianna knocked on his door.

"Is it too late to get married?" asked Hoyt.

"Well, I was about to close up," said the old man. He had scanty hair, combed across a bald pate and he was holding his shirt collar closed against the cool night air. He looked at them skeptically. "Do you have your marriage license and identification?"

"Yes, we do."

"Well…alright then. Come on in."

Hoyt handed over the marriage license and they both gave the man their driver licenses. Dianna held her breath as the official looked over hers, but he handed it back without comment. In short order, they found themselves exchanging vows in what used to be a dining room in front of an arched trellis covered with artificial flowers. At least the official's wife and her sister, the witnesses, made it seem like a wedding. They fussed over Dianna. One of them gave her an inexpensive little brooch, a gold-toned basket of flowers made of colorful glass stones.

"It's a bridal bouquet to remind you of your wedding day," she said.

The motel was nothing more than a strip of cabins with parking spaces in front of them. They kissed awkwardly and tried to make themselves comfortable in the strange room.

Dianna went into the bathroom first. She changed into a white lace gown that her friends had given her as a wedding gift. Hoyt was sitting in a chair when she came out and gasped at the sight of her. They kissed more ardently and then it was his turn to use the bathroom.

Nervously, Dianna pulled down the blind, turned out the lights and got into the sagging bed.

Naked in the darkness, Hoyt came out of the bathroom to join her. He walked toward the bed, crossing in front of the cheap window blind just as a car pulled into a parking space. The headlights caught him in perfect silhouette…with a huge erection.

Dianna bounded out of the bed in fear, ran into the bathroom and locked the door.

No amount of pleading could calm her down or get her to come out, although she finally did open the door a crack and throw his clothes out.

"Dianna, *please* stop crying. I'll take you back to Alicia's. We don't have to do this now; we can wait. I'll take you home…just come out, please."

Dianna didn't talk at all on the way home. Hoyt tried to pretend that everything was all right. He said they could plan a "real" honeymoon later.

It was quarter to twelve when they got to the corner near Alicia's house. Hoyt kissed her and said, "I love you, Dianna. Don't worry about tonight." He told her to call him the next day. He would call back, leaving a message with Alicia.

Clutching her things to her chest, Dianna jumped out of the truck and ran.

Two weeks had passed since the night of the pajama party.

"You've got to see him or *something*," said Alicia. "He's calling my house every day!"

"Shh, they'll hear you," said Dianna, pointing to her bedroom door.

"Well, what are you going to do?"

"I don't know," said Dianna. She was turning the little flower basket brooch over and over in her hand. "I don't want to see him; I know that."

"But you're *married* to him."

"I'm not sure I am. I lied about my age, Alicia."

"So what are you going to do?"

"I'm going to tell my mother tonight. I have no choice."

———

"What have you done?! You *tramp*!" yelled her father, swinging at her, knocking her down.

"Nothing! Nothing!" said Dianna, her arms up as a shield against his blows. "We just said some words and signed some papers! We didn't do anything, Daddy!"

"Frank! Stop!" said her mother, pulling him off. "Let her alone! Stop!"

Red-faced and eyes blazing, he backed away from her and tried to control his breathing.

I was a fool to think she wouldn't tell him, thought Dianna, cowering on the floor. *But that's what I am, a fool! I do one stupid thing after another!*

"We can talk about this in the morning, Frank!" said Betty, desperate to separate them.

"All right," he said at last, pushing her out the door. Looking at Dianna he said, "I'll deal with *you* in the morning." His voice dripped with disgust.

The door slammed shut.

Dianna spent the rest of the night crying and listening to them fight.

———

The next six months were a living hell for Dianna. Her sixteenth birthday came and went unremarked. Except for school, she was confined to her room, as before. Access to the family bathroom was the only reason she wasn't locked into it. No one was allowed to visit her.

Her father didn't believe her when she denied having sexual intercourse. He insisted on a gynecological exam. Dianna was terrified at the thought, so her mother set up an appointment with a female doctor, Elizabeth Merriam, to lessen her embarrassment. Dr. Merriam was very gentle with Dianna during the exam and confirmed her virginity to her parents.

"I don't believe her!" Frank railed when Betty told him the good news. "You women stick together! I want a second opinion…and *not* from a woman!"

So Dianna was forced to endure the humiliation of another internal exam, this time performed by Michael Shimberg, a male gynecologist. There was a sharp pain this time…and blood on the table. Dr. Shimberg confirmed Dr. Merriam's opinion.

At school, Dianna was a virtual pariah. Everyone knew about the elopement. Now she had no girlfriends at all, not even Alicia. There was one group who became *more* interested in her, though. This bunch made lascivious jokes in the corridors at her expense and whistled at her from their cars as she walked home from school.

And then came the day when Dianna and her parents went to court for the annulment of her marriage. Judge Shiela Townsend not only listened to the attorneys, she encouraged Dianna to explain what had happened. Dianna began with the skating and tearfully told the whole story. She was a "horrible girl"; she deserved to be kept in her room. She didn't blame her father for not speaking to her, for not believing she was a virgin. She was sorry, so sorry!

"When did you quit skating, Dianna?"

"About a year and a half ago, Your Honor," said Dianna, clutching a tissue.

A look came over the judge's face as she asked more detailed questions about Dianna's skating background. Every so often she asked Frank Wieland a question about his involvement in his daughter's skating and his feelings about that. Frank was glad that someone finally *understood* about Dianna's disobedience and her complete lack of gratitude.

Judge Townsend brought the questioning to a close and gave her ruling.

Because the marriage was not consummated and Dianna was under the age of consent, the annulment was granted.

But not before the judge gave Frank Wieland a serious dressing-down.

"For ten months you all but imprisoned your daughter, Mr. Wieland, simply because she didn't want to continue skating. By calling the parents of her friends, you even cut off any normal social contact your daughter might have had at school. What did you think would be the result of such draconian measures? Is this your idea of good parenting?"

Dianna's father was in shock.

Dianna's mother was sad, but not surprised.

Dianna…was in pieces.

27

Julie looked at Joe and saw the same look of pity that was in her own heart for this poor mother. Betty Wieland sat in between them in front of the battered shoebox. She wasn't crying. Julie thought that her tear ducts must be like a dry well, long since emptied.

"What did Frank do, Betty?" she asked gently. "Did he take it out on Dianna?"

"No," she said, shaking her head. "Frank really *did* love Dianna. He finally saw what condition she was in, what the whole mess had done to her. For the first time in almost two years I think he looked at her and saw how his beautiful daughter had been hurt.

"No, Frank didn't blame *her* anymore." She shook her head in disgust.

"It was *Hoyt* who was to blame for Dianna's devastation as far as Frank was concerned. Hoyt was the one who had to pay. Never mind that there was less than three years between them in age, never mind that he didn't have sex with Dianna, that he brought her right back when she asked him to, that, according to Dianna, it wasn't even his idea to go to New Hampshire and get married.

"Clearly Dianna and Alicia cooked-up the elopement. Dianna wanted to escape her home-life and Alicia wanted to help her. Hoyt was a 'knight in shining armor' who would rescue her! I daresay Hoyt saw himself that way, too."

"So what happened?" asked Joe.

"Frank insisted that we see an attorney, Marvin Gold, in Boston, who was recommended by one of his friends. I didn't want to go. We had known the Gellers, Hoyt's family, for years. I didn't want to prosecute poor Hoyt! What was to be gained by that? The lawyer said pretty much the same thing, too. He said that, '*in cases like these, the families usually just let it go*'." He called it a '*Romeo and Juliet*' thing, or something like that, because they were so close in age.

"Frank didn't want to hear anything like that, though! '*Can* I prosecute?' he asked. The lawyer asked if Dianna and Hoyt had engaged in sex. Right away I said that they didn't, that two doctors said she was a virgin. 'Those kids didn't even spend one night together!' I said.

"Frank told me to shut-up. He said that Hoyt was eighteen, that he was a '*man*'.

"Mr. Gold asked where the marriage had taken place and we told him New Hampshire. And then he said, 'In that case, you can prosecute him under the Mann Act. It's against Federal law to take a minor across a state line for immoral purposes.'

Hoyt was only two-and-a-half years older than Dianna! I pleaded with Frank not to pursue it, but it was useless. His own absolution was tied up in punishing Hoyt."

"Did Hoyt go to prison?" asked Joe.

Betty put her face in her hands. Her voice was barely audible.

"Yes, for seven years."

29

y Wieland wiped her eyes with a tissue and
 her hand on the shoebox.

and Joe leaned forward, listening intently.

se are letters Hoyt sent to Dianna," said Betty.
 few of them. You think your heart is broken
an't feel any more pain…and then you do.

 Red Cross called to see if we had any
 goods to donate, and I was going through
gs in our storage room. I noticed a cardboard
ad never unpacked from when we moved
k had stacked some cans of paint on top of
ved them. I dragged the box out into the
 tore it open. It looked like it was filled with
 but there were some things underneath. I
ting through them: old pictures of Frank in
 gear, a tarnished silver-plated trophy…and
x.

k was the one who brought the mail in every
ee. He was the one who paid the bills and

28

Massachusetts, 1997

Hoyt Geller peered through the grimy window of the bus. Dark gray clouds, heavy with moisture, stretched as far as he could see. A storm was coming. Birds lined-up on telephone wires, huddled together. They would fly away to shelter soon, to somewhere safe.

Hoyt had just turned nineteen. Furtively, he looked from one prisoner to the other, searching for a kindred spirit. There was none to be found; he had nothing in common with the older men aboard the bus but an orange jumpsuit and handcuffs. One of them, a big man with a shaved head and a gold tooth, caught him looking...and smiled.

Hoyt quickly lowered his eyes.

Too soon, the bus lumbered through a guarded gate, passage through a twelve-foot high chain link fence draped with razor wire. That fence would

separate him from all that was
next seven to ten years. The rea
As if to emphasize the point,
clanged together, closing behind

At a signal from the arme
and shuffled off the bus and
processed. The prisoners were
inside. The guards' voices seen
cement-block walls.

"Stay in line!"

"Over here, HERE!"

They pushed and they
moved along.

Hoyt wanted to cry, but he

And then they were in a
were forced to take off all thei
before everyone to be exami
himself; fear made him steal
had smiled at him on the
again...only this time he wasn

there was rarely anything for me. Obviously, he intercepted these letters from Hoyt and kept them hidden away all these years.

"I couldn't have been more shocked! Hoyt wasn't allowed to contact Dianna, of course. How did he manage to send letters to her? And, more important, why did Frank *save* them, why didn't he report them?

"It was *guilt*, I realized, pure and simple. Just like he was with Dianna, Frank was oblivious to the wreckage he'd made of Hoyt's life until it was too late…until he read his letters. Frank would never admit his guilt to anyone, mind you, but he couldn't bring himself to throw away a *single* letter.

Betty's chin trembled as she began to cry.

"I wanted to confront him, to throw them at him!" she cried. Taking a breath, she composed herself once again. "But I knew for sure that he would destroy them."

"So that was why you moved," said Joe.

"Yes. I realize now that Frank didn't want Hoyt to know where Dianna lived. The letters stopped when we moved here. There are none after that date."

"I'm *so* glad you brought them," said Julie. "Can you leave them with us?"

"Yes. I put everything back in the cardboard box in the storeroom and put the paint cans back on top," she said, rising from her seat. "It looks the same as it did before."

Quickly, she crossed the room, opening the office door. She turned back to face them.

"I don't know if the letters are important, but I know Dianna would want the whole truth to come out." And then she was gone, leaving one battered shoebox and two stunned investigators in her wake.

30

~~~~~

M ike Menello was trying to calm himself as he eased the big SUV into the curbside Downtown parking space. He felt anxious, like he had butterflies in his gut.

There's no way she could know for sure. That sleeping pill knocks her out cold; she wouldn't wake up if a bomb went off next to her. She never remembers anything, either.

Despite his confidence that Sabrina could not have known that he was absent that night, Mike was still a nervous wreck. Without her alibi he was up Shit Creek without a paddle. His life was literally hanging by a thread and Sabrina held the scissors.

Pushing the unsettling thought aside, he walked across West Robinson to the Mint Julep. Putting on his best face, he sauntered in and sat at the bar.

"Hey, Tony. Beautiful day! What's up?"

"Hi, Mike," said the bartender, a handsome frosted-blond guy. He was dressed head-to-toe in black, which was the uniform, day or night, in the Downtown bistro. "I don't usually see you this early. What can I get you? You want a lunch menu?"

"No. Nothing, thanks. I'm looking for Bo. Is he in?"

"Bo" was Robert Connolly, the owner of the Mint Julep.

"No. He had some business in Miami. I'm in charge today, that's why *I'm* in so early," he said. "He'll be here tomorrow night, upstairs. You coming in?"

"Yeah," said Mike, getting up. "That's good. Tell him I'll be here."

"Will do," said Tony with a wink.

The butterflies were subsiding by the time Mike Menello got back to his SUV. He was feeling a lot more hopeful about the whole situation.

———

Sabrina was putting together two copies of settlement papers for a buyer and a seller who were scheduled to arrive at her agency for a closing in thirty minutes. She slipped them into separate Nolen Title file folders.

It was a relief to have the distraction of work. Now that it was done, her worrisome thoughts drifted back to Mike. She sat back in her chair, her brow knit with concern. There was no point in kidding herself, she thought; she had fallen for the guy. Otherwise, she would have kicked him out.

Had he left her bed the night Dianna Wieland died? She honestly didn't know. But she did know that he'd done *exactly* that on another night...

31

"I'm next," said Gold Tooth.

"Shut up!" said the prisoner hurting Hoyt. "You're lucky you're here."

"Look at him crying!" said the third guy in the maintenance closet. "That's it, Baby, go ahead and cry, just like a girl!"

And Hoyt did.

They all laughed uproariously.

The guard outside stuck his head in.

"Quiet down, you perverts. And shut *him* up, too!" he said. "Five more minutes and that's it."

Shaking his head with disgust, the guard pulled the door closed again.

For the next several days, Hoyt kept his eyes on the floor, not daring to make eye contact with anyone. Every so often one of the other prisoners would call him "Baby" and laugh.

A skinny blond guy, a head shorter than Hoyt, threw him a sympathetic glance.

Hoyt sat at the end of a bench in the cafeteria trying to eat some horrible stew, hoping Gold Tooth and the other two men didn't come anywhere near him. He was terrified. What was he to do? Tell the warden? Then he'd be dead.

He breathed a sigh of relief when Benny Dahlgren sat next to him.

Benny was a thirty-five year old divorce lawyer who got involved with a client. He and his client ended up killing the client's wife. Both men were serving life sentences in different correctional institutions.

"You okay, Hoyt?" he asked quietly.

"Yeah," said Hoyt, hoping Benny would drop the subject.

"A kid before you...he hung himself with some shoelaces," said Benny.

Hoyt almost choked on the mystery meat in his stew.

They ate quietly for a while.

"They'd stop if you were with me," said Benny under his breath, picking up his tray. "And I'd never force you to do anything."

Hoyt swallowed hard and turned, looking at Benny wide-eyed.

In the same low-key voice, Benny said, "Eat your lunch and don't look so scared. I'm not like them; you wouldn't have to do that again. I'd take good care of you. I've got a lot of connections. Think about it. I like you, Hoyt, but only if you want to do it."

And then he was gone.

It didn't take long to decide that Benny beat shoelaces.

32

"This 'Hoyt Geller' who went to prison back then could be our killer," said Joe.

"I don't know," said Julie, shaking her head. "It sounds like he loved Dianna to me."

"Yeah…*past tense*. A guy could get bitter sitting in jail for seven years. From what Betty said, it sounds like he's out now. I'll look into that today."

"Even so, we shouldn't jump to conclusions. Let's read the letters."

She pulled her chair up to his as he pulled one out.

"Wait, check the date," said Julie. "We should read them in order, don't you think?"

"Right," said Joe, looking at the postmarks. "Okay…they're filed front to back." He pulled the first one out and slid the letter out of its envelope. There were two neatly written pages on white, lined paper:

29

B etty Wieland wiped her eyes with a tissue and put her hand on the shoebox.

Julie and Joe leaned forward, listening intently.

"These are letters Hoyt sent to Dianna," said Betty. "I read a few of them. You think your heart is broken and you can't feel any more pain…and then you do.

"The Red Cross called to see if we had any household goods to donate, and I was going through some things in our storage room. I noticed a cardboard box we had never unpacked from when we moved here. Frank had stacked some cans of paint on top of it. I removed them. I dragged the box out into the garage and tore it open. It looked like it was filled with old towels but there were some things underneath. I started sorting through them: old pictures of Frank in his hockey gear, a tarnished silver-plated trophy…and this shoebox.

"Frank was the one who brought the mail in every day, you see. He was the one who paid the bills and separate him from all that was normal in life for the next seven to ten years. The reality of it was crushing. As if to emphasize the point, the chain link gates clanged together, closing behind the bus.

At a signal from the armed guard, they all stood and shuffled off the bus and into the building to be processed. The prisoners were silent, yet it was noisy inside. The guards' voices seemed to echo off the gray cement-block walls.

"Stay in line!"

"Over here, HERE!"

They pushed and they shoved as each man moved along.

Hoyt wanted to cry, but he didn't.

And then they were in a cold room where they were forced to take off all their clothes and stand naked before everyone to be examined. Hoyt couldn't help himself; fear made him steal a glance at the man who had smiled at him on the bus. Gold Tooth smiled again…only this time he wasn't looking at Hoyt's face.

28

Massachusetts, 1997

Hoyt Geller peered through the grimy window of the bus. Dark gray clouds, heavy with moisture, stretched as far as he could see. A storm was coming. Birds lined-up on telephone wires, huddled together. They would fly away to shelter soon, to somewhere safe.

Hoyt had just turned nineteen. Furtively, he looked from one prisoner to the other, searching for a kindred spirit. There was none to be found; he had nothing in common with the older men aboard the bus but an orange jumpsuit and handcuffs. One of them, a big man with a shaved head and a gold tooth, caught him looking…and smiled.

Hoyt quickly lowered his eyes.

Too soon, the bus lumbered through a guarded gate, passage through a twelve-foot high chain link fence draped with razor wire. That fence would

150

Hoyt was only two-and-a-half years older than Dianna! I pleaded with Frank not to pursue it, but it was useless. His own absolution was tied up in punishing Hoyt."

"Did Hoyt go to prison?" asked Joe.

Betty put her face in her hands. Her voice was barely audible.

"Yes, for seven years."

Dear Dianna,

I miss you so much! I miss being at home with my Mom and Dad, too. I feel terrible for what I've done to them. But at least they can visit me. I wish you could! Please don't worry about me and don't feel bad. What happened is MY fault because I'm older. I should have known about that law. It sounds stupid – it WAS stupid - but I always thought of New Hampshire more like the next town, not a separate state, you know what I mean?

(I have to tell you something - I know we both felt bad about how things turned out that night, but now I THANK GOD we didn't do it. What if you got pregnant and they sent me away? That would have been much, much worse.)

Anyway, DON'T WORRY ABOUT ME. I have a friend now and he looks out for me. He says he can get this letter out. He's been here a long time and I'm not going to say his name, just in case somebody else gets it. I made up the girl's name on the return address so your parents won't know this is from me. God knows I don't want to get you in any more trouble! If nothing happens, I'll know you got it and I'll write you again!

I love you, Dianna. Thinking of you is the ONE thing that can get me through this. I know you can't write me but I hope you love me, too.

I pray to God that this reaches you.

Love,

Hoyt

"A 'friend' who 'looks out' for him," said Joe. "Geez. Do you know what that means, Julie? Nobody does favors for nothing in prison. Poor guy…"

33

Massachusetts, 1998

"You've got to stop thinking about the outside, Hoyt," said Benny. "You're never going to make it through if you don't."

"It's only four months and it feels like four years."

Benny took off his glasses and rubbed the bridge of his nose. He was an average looking man, about as tall as Hoyt, with short, wiry, dark hair. Benny had never been happier since the beginning of his sentence. He didn't take Hoyt's comment personally. For Benny, Hoyt was a dream come true; he didn't want him to be unhappy.

"Why don't you write Dianna again? We would have heard about it by now if she didn't get your letter."

"It's not too soon?" asked Hoyt, a new light in his eyes.

"No. Here's what you do. Take a few days to think about what you want to say and then write her a nice long letter. I'll get it mailed for you."

It killed Benny to think that Hoyt was in love with Dianna Wieland, but, at the end of the day, it didn't matter. Hoyt would be happy for awhile…and grateful.

Dear Dianna,

I hope you went back to school and everything is all right with your mother and father. I miss you SO much. I think about you every day and every night. My friend says I should stop thinking about life outside of the prison because it makes the time here go slower. I know he's right…except for YOU.

I'm going to ask my mother and father not to come here so often. At first, I couldn't wait to see them, especially my mother. But now, it just makes it harder to be in here. They can write me letters. I wish you could write me…but DON'T…you'll get us both in trouble and I won't be able to write.

I miss my horse, Fitzie. His whole name is Fitzwarren. Crazy name, huh? My parents bought him at an auction for my eighth birthday. He was eight years old, too. Maybe you can't teach "an old dog new tricks", but Fitzie is really smart. I taught him a lot of wonderful tricks. I hate to think that he's probably going to die while I'm in here. Anyway, that's the kind of thing I shouldn't be thinking about. I've just got to adapt to being in here. My friend says the time will go by faster if I do that.

But how can I stop thinking about you? I close my eyes and pretend I'm with you. It's the only way I can go on. Do you think about me, Dianna? About the time we had together? Do you remember? Do you miss me like I miss you?

I'll write you once a month!
Love,
Hoyt

Hoyt carefully folded the letter and put it in his shoe. He lay on his bunk, hands entwined on his chest, looking up at the dark gray cement ceiling. His mind projected Dianna's warm face on the cold stone surface. He closed his eyes to see her better. When sleep came, she bent to kiss him, her dark hair falling around the two of them like a warm cocoon.

One day passed like another in a monotonous atmosphere punctuated by anger and brutality. Hoyt, as Benny had predicted, was not bothered anymore by the other inmates, who respected Benny and relied on him for answers to their legal questions. Even the guards stepped carefully around Benny…and Hoyt, by extension.

The fact was that Hoyt actually liked Benny. It was good to have a friend and he benefited from their conversations. Benny knew everything that was going on in the correctional facility, which the inmates called the "Department of Corruption". He helped Hoyt navigate the sea of convicts and the men who guarded them.

Their relationship was only a problem when Benny began to touch him.

And then the actor took over…and the real Hoyt left with Dianna.

The weirdest thing to accept was that Hoyt was considered a "sexual offender".

Because he was convicted under the Mann Act, he was automatically enrolled in the "Sex Offender Treatment Program" and forced to spend days at a time in group sessions with a dozen other men serving time for sexual offenses. Their slyness and their stories sickened him to the point of nausea. Being grouped with them shamed him.

Oddly enough, it was Benny who understood and helped him cope with the unfairness of the situation. If anyone knew what a naïve, straight-arrow Hoyt was, it was Benny.

"Just go along with it, Hoyt. You stay out of trouble, serve the minimum time, and you'll be a free man. You won't have to see any of that scum again. You're not like any of them…you're not even like me."

Hoyt looked at him almost apologetically.

"Oh, it's okay. I know the score, Hoyt. You can't help it. You're not wired to love me. It doesn't matter; I love you, anyway. No matter what your circumstances are, having someone to love makes life worth living," said Benny. "Write Dianna another letter, my friend."

Dear Dianna,

Everything is upside down in here...right is wrong and wrong is right. The ONLY thing that helps me keep it all straight is you. I would lose my SELF without you. I just do everything they say and be respectful, so I can get out of here in as few years as possible. YEARS. I can barely stand to write that!

Where will you be then?

My friend says I shouldn't think of that, so I won't talk about that anymore.

Have you been to the beach yet? I used to go to Hampton Beach in New Hampshire all the time. I wish I could go to the beach with you. We never went anywhere - but that's all right. Someday we WILL go to the beach. We'll go everywhere, just you and me. PLEASE wait for me, Dianna. I love you so much. I'll hold you in my heart until I can hold you in my arms,

Hoyt

34

~

"It's so sad to think of what happened to this young man," said Julie. "These three letters are heartbreaking, Joe."

"You said it. Worse, he sounds so *young,* like a teenager."

"He *was* a teenager when he wrote most of these," said Julie. "He was nineteen, I believe."

"I can't help thinking about something Betty said, something about '*Romeo and Juliet*'," said Joe. "That's what these two were like."

"Not exactly," said Julie, thumbing through the letters. "Remember, this was a lopsided love affair; Dianna was too young. I'm sure she cared about Hoyt, but her primary motivation was escaping from her father," said Julie. "There's nine more letters, Joe. Why don't I read the next five and you read the remaining four. Let's see if they're all in the same vein."

"Good idea."

They split them up and began to read. A few minutes later, Joe said, "Whoa," and laid a letter in front of Julie. "Look at this…"

Dear Dianna,

I want to write about all good things, but there isn't anything good happening here. A prisoner killed himself last night. It happened in his cell and I didn't see him - but news gets around. His name was Bernie or Barney, I think. I saw him in the cafeteria the other day.

He should have been in a mental hospital. He yelled, 'There's a big rat! He's going to eat me!' They got him settled down, but he must have acted up again later. I heard they put him in isolation. I don't think he could obey the rules because I don't think he knew what they were.

Anyway, he stuck a plastic knife in his neck. I guess he thought it was better than being eaten by the rat.

Love,

Hoyt

"Oh-oh, that's bad. He's deteriorating," said Julie. "The ones *I* have are all love letters. Were the letters before that one anything like it?"

"Maybe a little more self-pity, but *nothing* as extreme as that. And here," said Joe, handing her another one, "look at the last letter, Merlin, it's even worse."

Julie took the letter and began to read…

Dear Dianna,
I told you in my last letter about a man who killed himself. We had another one last week. Nobody can remember his name. He was a drug addict - it was only his third day here. He was twitching and sweating – everybody could see he was sick. He tore a strip off his sheet and hung himself from the smoke alarm in his cell. They found him in the morning.

He didn't have to die – somebody should have checked on him.

I'm so tired. I keep dreaming about Crazy Man with a knife in his neck and Sick Man hanging. In my dream, I'm in a long line of men marching past the dead men in their cells – but I'm the only one who looks at them.

I HATE THIS PLACE.
I'm sorry,
Hoyt

"No wonder Frank Wieland was so anxious to move," said Julie. "The change in tone is frightening."

Joe nodded, thoughtfully.

"It's plain to see that he was traumatized by the deaths."

"We need to see if he's out of prison, Joe."

He was already punching a number into his phone.

"Way ahead of you, Merlin."

35

The killer watched himself getting dressed in the mirror over his dresser. He began to button his shirt, one by one, from the top down. In his mind, he spoke to his own image:

At least I stopped O'Hara from coming around. That was damn risky, but what else could I do? She was a much bigger threat than the detective, Garrett.

Lately, he'd been troubled by another loose end.

Several cars had passed by while he'd sat in the SUV that morning before Dianna came out of the condo. Because of the tinted windows, he didn't think anyone could have seen him; it was his ride he was worried about. Besides Dianna's Lexus, his SUV was the only other vehicle in that area...and it was parked right next to her car.

He fretted about it as he combed his hair.

What if some passerby remembered?

He had to get his nerves under control. He was worrying about nothing! No one had come forward about that and Dianna's death was no longer front-page news.

I hope the hell it stays that way...

He took a last look, straightened his collar, and went out the door.

36

Sabrina Nolen hated taking prescription drugs of any kind and had eliminated all of them but her sleeping meds. In recent months, she had tried to wean herself off them by cutting them in half. Her attempts were unsuccessful. Although the half-dose induced sleep, it didn't last through the night and she woke up. On one of those occasions, her eyes had popped open and Mike Menello was missing from her bed.

Presuming he was in the bathroom, Sabrina had waited patiently for him to come out so she could go get the other half of her sleeping pill. After a time, she decided to go knock on the door. To her surprise, he wasn't in there. She thought he must be in the kitchen getting a snack, so she went ahead and took the other half of her pill and got back in bed. But the darkness of the house and the quiet began to bother her.

Was he out by the pool? Was he all right?

There was no way she could get to sleep like that! Aggravated, she'd gotten up and gone through the

173

house looking for him, finally checking out the garage. The SUV was gone.

At one in the morning! The son-of-bitch was probably screwing around on her!

Sabrina had been angry about it, but the hypnotic pill had begun to take effect and she'd gone back to bed. In the morning, her head was cooler and she tried to trap him in a lie. He was sitting in the kitchen when she walked in.

"Good morning," he said. "How did you sleep?"

"I slept good," she said. "How about *you?*"

"As a matter of fact, I had a headache that wouldn't quit. I had to go out and get some Excedrin Migraine. I drove all around the place trying to find a drugstore that was open."

Reassured, Sabrina had kissed him on the cheek and put the incident out of her mind.

Until she became his alibi for *another* night.

For the last week, Sabrina had delayed taking her medicine and pretended to be asleep. Mike had slept right through each night, unaware of her vigil. Last night, she had finally gone to sleep after taking her medication at two o'clock.

Now she awoke to bright sunlight slicing through the vertical blinds in her bedroom and striking her face. Mike was up and gone. Squinting and groggy, she swung her legs out of the bed and picked up the clock, trying to focus on the numbers without her glasses.

Twenty past ten.

How long am I going to do this? I can't keep this up.

She pulled on her robe and her slippers and padded into the kitchen. The coffee was cold, so she dumped it out and made a fresh pot. She thought about Mike as she waited for it to brew.

It was a difficult situation because Sabrina was in love with him. But facts were facts. Mike had had an irrational hatred for Dianna Wieland and had blamed her for conspiring against him. Now she was dead and Sabrina was his alibi. The only problem was that she didn't believe him.

She loved him, but Mike was a habitual liar. If she came right out and accused him it could end their relationship.

Sabrina poured herself a cup of coffee, added some cream and took it out to the table by the pool. She sat in the shade, her feet propped up on a second chair, cradling the cup in her hands.

One more night. I have to know where he's going.

———

It was a quarter to one in the morning and Sabrina was right behind Mike. She was inside the laundry room at the door leading into the garage, waiting to hear the outside automatic door close. The moment it did, she stepped into the garage and hit the door opener. She was counting on him not to notice the door rise again as he drove down the hill.

Mike exited the subdivision and turned right. Sabrina waited just long enough to put some space between them. He took another right at the light and she followed him onto Apopka-Vineland Road. Before long, they were on headed northeast on Interstate 4.

Where the hell is he going? Downtown? Winter Park?

Even though the traffic was light, it was hard to follow the black SUV at night. Sabrina had to stay quite close, but she thought that it would be equally hard for him to see anything but her headlights behind him.

Downtown. He's getting off. Careful! Don't lose him...

Oh, God. Oh, God. He's going to Lake Eola.

Sabrina kept on going and drove past Mike as he pulled the SUV in next to Eola Park Center. She turned the corner and quickly did a U-turn. When she came back, she spotted him walking up Robinson. She pulled out and slowly followed.

Didn't they say her car was parked right near here? Oh, God.

Where is he going?

And then he was crossing the street, stopping at a door. It looked like a restaurant...

Oh, yes, the Mint Julep.

I've heard of it.

But what is he doing? It's closed...

To Sabrina's complete shock, the door opened and Mike went in.

37

Julie's leg was killing her. The long, emotional day had taken its toll. And it wasn't just her broken leg; her underarms were sore from the crutches and her lower back hurt like hell.

She was sitting, propped-up in her bed with the shoebox full of Hoyt Geller's letters to Dianna at her side. She punched and pushed the pillows behind her, trying to get more comfortable. Sol was lying on the floor beside the bed. She called to him, patting the space next to her on the bed.

"C'mon up, Sol. C'mon, handsome! Come up here next to me."

The huge cat didn't even bother to lift his head.

"That's nice, Sol. I feel like crap and I want to pat you, and you completely ignore me. You're the reason people have dogs."

She turned her attention again to the letters she'd been studying.

There was such a paradigm shift between Hoyt's first letters and his last. What had taken her and Joe by surprise was the suddenness of the change. Julie was certain that it was the inmate suicides that had tipped the scale. She thought that, up until then, thinking about Dianna had given Hoyt *hope.*

Sighing, she pushed the letters aside and reached over to turn off the lamp.

As she lay there in the dark, her thoughts traveled back through the years to a deteriorating young man in a prison cell.

How does anyone live without hope?

38

Massachusetts, 1999

Hoyt had been in the Men's Correctional Facility for seventeen months and twelve days. Besides the two suicides, there had been another death that the prison officials referred to as a "bizarre accident". Hoyt was hard-pressed to think of swallowing a light bulb as any kind of an accident, bizarre or otherwise.

Benny had pulled some strings and they were now housed together in a two bunk cell.

"The last one came back, Hoyt," said Benny, handing him a letter.

"No."

"Yes, it did. My friend went to mail this one and the other one was returned to the post office box. They must have moved, Hoyt."

"You're lying. You're lying! You don't want me to write her anymore!"

"Keep your voice down. I'm not lying."

"Yes, you are. You want me to forget about Dianna."

"Yes, I do, but I'm not lying about the letter being returned," said Benny. "Listen, Hoyt. Hanging on to Dianna like a life preserver isn't good for you. You need to toughen up and learn to swim without her or *anybody* on the outside, or *you'll never do the time*. This was bound to happen, sooner or later. We were lucky we didn't get caught smuggling these letters out."

"So that's it," said Hoyt. "You don't want to get caught."

"Oh, come on. What's going to happen to me? Nothing. But *you*? A 'sexual offender' writing love letters to his 'victim'? They'll add to your time, Hoyt, and you'll be spending even more hours with the scumbag-molesters getting 'rehabilitated'!"

Hoyt knew Benny was right. He hadn't been able to picture Dianna clearly for the last couple of months. He didn't even know what to write anymore. He tried to think "I love you" but it came out "I hate this place". He'd felt dead inside for weeks, hopeless. He hadn't been talking to Benny. And Benny had let him alone.

That was good of him…

For the first time since he was assaulted, the tears rose up inside of Hoyt and burst through the dam he'd constructed. Desolate, he put his face in his hands and his shoulders shook with the loss. And then Benny was there with his arms around him.

"It'll be easier, Hoyt, I promise you."

39

Massachusetts, 2002

The inmates in Doctor Edwin Frommer's rehab group were a particularly egregious bunch of sex offenders. Almost to the man, they were faking rehabilitation and marking time until they could get out. It was, therefore, not surprising that they showed little interest in "Pets for a Purpose." PP was a new program designed to help inmates become "other centered" by rehabilitating shelter dogs or training special dogs to assist the blind and disabled.

The psychiatrist was also not surprised by the *one* inmate who did volunteer.

"Doctor Frommer," said Hoyt, hanging back after the rest had all trooped out, "could I volunteer for the dog training program?"

Ed Frommer had been working with sexually deviant inmates for ten years and he was absolutely certain that Hoyt Geller wasn't one of them. In his opinion, it was damaging for Hoyt to be in their company.

There was a light in the young man's eyes that the doctor hadn't seen in a long time.

"Why do you want to do this, Hoyt?"

"I could do a good job, Dr. Frommer. I grew up on a farm. I'm good with animals."

Frommer smiled. He thought the program would be a wonderful escape for Hoyt.

"I think you'd be good at it, too, Hoyt. I'm going to recommend you for the program. It will conflict with the group, but we'll continue our work on an individual basis."

"You mean I'm not going to be in the group anymore?" said Hoyt, wide-eyed, not believing his good fortune.

"No," said Dr. Frommer, "not as long as you're in that program."

And so, on April 15, 2002, while everyone on the outside was scrambling to get their income taxes done, Hoyt was introduced to Cisco, a rambunctious, two-year old German Shepherd mix…and hell became a lot more bearable.

———

It was a beautiful day in early June and Hoyt almost felt free. Training Cisco outside, along with the other inmates and their charges, was the best part of Hoyt's day. For awhile, focusing on his bond with the dog, he could forget the chain link and razor wire that tied the deep green lawn to the pale blue sky.

At the end of the week, Cisco would be gone. Hoyt would sorely miss him, but he was happy for him at the same time, because the animal had become an alter-ego of sorts.

Cisco was a "problem dog" who had ended up in a shelter. He loved people, but didn't know how to behave around them. In his exuberance, Cisco would jump on them and knock them down. When they took him for a walk, it was like being in a horse-and-buggy…without the buggy.

Because of Hoyt's love and consistent training, Cisco was a changed dog. All Hoyt had to do was give a hand signal and say "Down stay" and Cisco would drop to the ground and not move. It no longer mattered what was going on around him; Cisco's eyes were on his master. The German Shepherd wanted nothing more than to please Hoyt and was happily enjoying all the praise heaped upon him for doing so. Soon, he would be following the same commands for someone else in the surrounding community, who would love him and give him a good home.

Cisco would be paroled. He would be reconnected to society.

He would have a second chance at life.

Hoyt's meetings with Dr. Frommer, only once a week now, were entirely different than the rehab group meetings. Hoyt was never specific about Benny, but, somehow, he felt that Frommer knew and understood the compromise he had made. They talked about a lot of things…and sometimes they talked about women. It was good. It made Hoyt feel that he hadn't *changed*, that he was still a regular guy, just currently on *hold*.

Talking to Frommer helped him deal with prison life, in general. Instead of looking at incarceration as his *life*, the way Benny did, Hoyt began to look at it as an *interim period* in his life. It had a beginning, a middle part, and an end…and Hoyt was coming up on the *end*.

Benny was a nagging problem for him, though. A sensitive and intelligent man, he was growing more and more disconsolate as Hoyt's term neared completion. Try as he might, Hoyt couldn't see anyone in the prison population who would be a good match for his friend. Hoyt thought that this would always be the case inside for someone like Benny, who had been alone before Hoyt came along and probably would be again. Because of his concern, he decided to talk about it with Dr. Frommer.

"So, I'm really a little worried about how he's going to cope with being alone," said Hoyt. "He's gotten attached to me, you know, Doc?"

"I do, indeed, Hoyt," said Dr. Frommer, thoughtfully. "Do you think it would help if Benny could get into the Pets for a Purpose program?"

"Yes!" said Hoyt. "I think that would be great!"

"Well, you'll have to get him to come in and volunteer," said Frommer. "If he does, I'll recommend him for the program."

"He's almost ready to graduate into the real world," said Hoyt. He was referring to Blackie, a Lab-Collie mix that Benny had been training for several weeks.

"Yeah...like you," said Benny.

Hoyt was scheduled to be released the next day, his seven year service at an end.

Benny smiled, putting on a brave front in spite of his sadness. "You know, Hoyt, I have to thank you for getting me into this program. I like being around the dogs. Everybody is nicer, even the guards."

"That's true," said Hoyt, stroking his current charge, Biscuit, a Golden Retriever. "They can't help but feel the love. You treat a dog right and he'll love you unconditionally...unlike people."

Unbidden, Dianna Wieland's banished face came to mind.

"That's how I feel about you, Hoyt," said Benny.

Hoyt's feelings for Benny were complex. In retrospect, it boiled down to one thing, though: In a cage full of brutes, two reasonable men had accommodated each other's needs. But now it was over, and though Benny would be desolate for awhile, Hoyt couldn't wait to be done with the physical aspect of their relationship, infrequent though it was. He had forced Dianna from his mind but he had replaced her with mental images of other women. It was the only way he'd been able cope with his bizarre situation.

"I know, Benny. I'll miss you, too," he said, delivering the expected line with sincerity worthy of an

Academy Award. He was privately thrilled that the curtain was falling. When he walked through the prison gates, Hoyt planned to enjoy as many women as possible and never think of Benny again.

40

Massachusetts, 2004

It was a sunny autumn day and the Geller's beat-up Ford F-150 truck was parked outside the correctional facility. Rolf and his wife, Katrin, stood in front of the pickup waiting for their only child. They were unsophisticated German immigrants in their sixties who still spoke with a heavy accent. Katrin, a short, stocky woman with gray hair pulled back in a thick ponytail, stood with her hands nervously clasped together. Her husband was her opposite in appearance, a man with thinning pale blond hair, tall and tanned from long summer hours of farm work. He paced back and forth, his hands clasped behind his back.

He turned at the sound of a guard escorting a prisoner to the gate and unlocking it.

The Gellers had said goodbye to a callow nineteen year-old boy, but it was a twenty-six year old man with a beard who walked toward them. At Hoyt's request, they hadn't been to visit him for six months…he didn't have the beard then, and the difference was striking.

"Mother…Father…it's good to see you," said Hoyt.

Rolf swallowed and Katrin began to cry.

Hoyt put his arms around both of them and hugged them tightly.

"Happy birthday, Hoyt," said his father, handing him the keys to a 1999 Toyota Camry. The five year old car had 70,000 miles on it, and there was nothing in Hoyt's limited world that could have made his twenty-seventh birthday happier.

Unable to get any kind of work nearby, Hoyt had been tied to the North Street farm…and to his parents. He wouldn't tell them immediately, but his intention was to land a job further away and move out. The car made it possible.

Maybe that's why they're giving it to me. They would never say it, but they've gotten used to living in this house by themselves.

Conversation with his parents was difficult…stilted and uncomfortable. Hoyt would retreat to his childhood bedroom, which had begun to feel every bit like the cell he had occupied for seven years. And he wasn't really needed on the farm. Four years ago, his father had hired a young man from Maine as a full-time hand. The guy lived in an apartment nearby and had become like an adopted son to them. It was clear that his father was not going to let him go.

I'm glad he's here. It makes it easier to leave.

———

"I'm sorry, Hoyt," said the sales manager. "I have to let you go. You lied on your employment application."

"Only because I couldn't get a damn job!" said Hoyt.

"I understand, but there's nothing I can do," the manager said.

It was plain to see that he was no longer enthusiastic about having Hoyt as an employee.

Hoyt signed the "Exit Interview" form, pushed it toward his ex-boss and left, toppling his chair in the process. He was so angry, he didn't stop to pick it up. He stormed out to his car and got in, whipping out of the parking lot onto the road leading to Interstate 95…and the farm.

Two damn weeks of driving all over creation for those assholes! I was on straight commission…I wasn't even costing them anything!

Under the circumstances, Hoyt knew he'd never collect a dime on the two sales he'd made for the farm equipment supplier.

He'd be twenty-eight soon. It was almost a year since he got the Camry he was driving! Being an ex-con wasn't supposed to make any difference to an employer. What a joke that was.

Will I ever be able to get a job? Will I have to spend the rest of my life working on the farm with my parents?

At times like this, it was hard not to blame Dianna for ruining his life. He'd heard that the Wielands had moved to Orlando, Florida.

I'm screwed and she's living in the land of fun and sun.

———

Losing the sales job was so depressing that Hoyt gave up looking for awhile, but eventually the need to live on his own motivated him to try again. This time the jobs he went for didn't involve a written application that could rule him out or come back to bite him.

At last, Hoyt was hired by a company called Boyer Landscape Service to cut lawns in the summer and plow snow in the winter. Even though the pay was terrible, Hoyt figured he could save up enough to move because he still worked on the farm and lived rent-free.

He was in his room counting his savings from five weeks of work, when he heard the pounding on the front door downstairs. He went to the top of the staircase. Uniformed policemen were trooping in, pushing past his mother and father.

"What's going on?" he said, running down the stairs.

"Hoyt Geller?" a cop asked.

"Yes. What do you want?"

"You're coming with us. Hands behind your back!"

They shoved him against the wall and clamped handcuffs on him.

"What are you doing?!" said Rolf Geller. "Where are you taking him?"

"He's going to the police station. We have some questions for him."

With no more explanation, they put Hoyt in the back of a cruiser and took him to police headquarters. There, they grilled him for three hours about a little girl in a neighboring town who had gone missing. After that they threw him in a jail cell. The next afternoon, they pushed him into a line-up.

Hoyt was on the Sexual Offenders List.

A local newspaper picked up the story and Boyer Landscape promptly fired him.

41

Massachusetts, 2006

He had given up all hope of a life apart from the farm. He would have to notify the Registry of Sexual Offenders of any move to any other city or state. He had been cruelly reminded that he was a *permanent* suspect.

Hoyt had come to accept the fact that he would never be truly free.

If he had learned anything from seven years behind bars it was this: There was no point in torturing himself with unattainable dreams. At least he wasn't a pariah here. His parents loved him, his co-worker was his friend, and there was a girl he'd met during the apple harvest last fall who was accommodating and didn't care about his reputation.

It's better than prison.

Hoyt smiled at the hired hand next to him, who was also holding tight to the truck, bouncing along in the back with all their tools and supplies.

It was a sunny day in April and they were circling the farm, checking the fence for winter damage. Rolf Geller was at the wheel navigating the rutted, hairpin road on the rear perimeter of the property which led to the top of Stripe Hill. Katrin had come along for the ride and had brought lunch. The woods on either side of the road were strewn with granite boulders, and the last of the melting snow on higher ground created little waterfalls and rills as it coursed over and between them.

The road dead-ended at a narrow access road at the top and Rolf Geller turned sharp right onto it and stopped. The view was wide open and spectacular, but they were all used to it and paid it no mind.

"The fence is sagging over there, Father," said Hoyt, pointing to a section of chain-link behind the truck on the left side of the access road.

"Okay. Stay there. I'll back up," said Rolf.

Somehow he stepped on the gas before he put the truck into reverse.

The next thing Hoyt knew they were shooting forward, crashing through chain-link, airborne over the granite quarry below. He tried to hold on, but he couldn't. The truck listed right from the heavy equipment and he went flying out of the bed along with it.

Tumbling…WHAM! Hoyt found himself on his back. He was stunned; he shook his head to clear it

Someone was screaming.

The pick-up was on fire! Not a fireball like in the movies... but it will be!

Jumping from rock to rock, he raced down the incline to the passenger door.

"MOTHER!"

Katrin was burning. They were all burning…and no one was screaming anymore.

Hoyt grabbed for his mother anyway, but flames raced up his left arm.

He fell back, pulling off his burning jacket and scrambling far away from the horror of the now fully engulfed truck.

Numb from shock, Hoyt sat staring at the blazing truck.

Why wasn't anybody coming?

Then he realized it was Sunday. No one was at the quarry.

The shock was wearing off and suddenly he felt tremendous pain in his left hand. He cried out as he raised it, palm up, to look. It was red and blistered.

Not charred…that's good…got to get home.

⸺

The climb out of the quarry was difficult, but not as bad as the trek to the farmhouse. The more time that passed, the more unbearable the pain became. Hoyt stumbled into the house and climbed the stairs, crying all the way.

He went directly to his parents' medicine cabinet. He was looking for a pain reliever that was prescribed for his father after shoulder surgery. Just recently, his father had been talking about it, how it made him "dizzy", how he "only took it for one day"…the name was *oxy*-something. Hoyt searched frantically through the medicines.

There…Oxycontin.

He took one and then stuck his hand under cold water.

"OW!"

He yanked the hand out, unable to bear the pain.

Infection. Burns get infected.

He found some gauze and gingerly dried his hand. Then he spread an antibacterial ointment all over it, wincing and grimacing in pain. Finally, he wrapped it loosely in the gauze. Breathing hard, he sat down on the toilet seat.

His Mother's bathrobe hung on a hook on the wall.

The pain of losing them ripped through Hoyt again and he sat there for an hour, crying convulsively, unable to do anything else. Finally his sobbing eased and he went into their room and lay down on their bed. His painful, pulsing hand woke him three hours later. He took another Oxycontin, returned to their bed and slept once again.

When the sun came up, Hoyt dragged himself to his feet. His whole body was bruised and hurting. But his hand….it throbbed so painfully it felt like a horrible alien thing…something apart from his body. He took another pill and sat on their bed.

His grief was profound; Hoyt had nothing left, not even a friend.

What did he have to live for?

He should have been the one to die with his parents.

42

<hr/>

"I'm going to lunch, Janet," said Joe, as he grabbed his keys and headed for the door.

"I might not be back this afternoon; I've got to talk to Merlin. I'll call you."

"Okay, Boss."

Joe quickly crossed the foyer between the two offices and walked into Julie's.

"Hi," he said, "is she busy?"

"No doubt," said Luz, "but nobody's in there with her."

"Okay, thanks," said Joe, going down the hall.

Julie was at her computer working on her manuscript, *Clues.* The editor had called Julie's agent to put pressure on Julie to either approve or correct the recent galleys sent by the publisher. Julie felt rather guilt-ridden that she'd let it go so long…and now here was Joe. When would she get this done?

"Hi," she said. "What's up?"

"He's dead."

"Who's dead?"

"Hoyt Geller," said Joe, handing her a fax. It was a copy of a Boston Globe newspaper article dated Tuesday, April 10, 2006:

Middlesex County
THREE KILLED IN
QUARRY CRASH

Quarry workers arriving for work on Monday found the smoking body of a Ford truck which had crashed through a chain link fence high up on a neighboring farm. The driver and two passengers were killed in the crash. They have been identified as Rolf Geller, 65, his wife, Katrin, 62, and their son, Hoyt, 28.

The Gellers owned the adjacent apple orchards and were apparently repairing fencing above the quarry. The disposition of North Street Farm was not immediately available.

The crash is under investigation.

"Oh, my God…that poor family."

"Yeah, it is sad," said Joe. "Seems like bad luck was the only kind they had. Anyway, that takes Hoyt Geller out of the equation, Merlin."

"Yes."

"So where do we go from here?"

Julie rubbed her forehead, thinking.

"To Sabrina Nolen."

43

Expecting Sabrina's resistance to another meeting, they decided that Julie should go alone. Joe would drop her off, crutches and all, at Nolen Title, killing time in the area himself until Julie called him to pick her up. They had deliberately timed the unannounced visit just prior to the lunch hour. Once again, Sabrina was in the middle of a closing and Julie took a seat in the anteroom and perused the magazines.

Before long, Sabrina came out of the conference room leading eight people, everyone carrying folders. It looked like a class of some type, but it was actually a set of parents and their adult children who were jointly purchasing property, along with the sellers and two real estate agents. Sabrina was giving them her usual congratulations and reassurance.

Julie was bracing for a swift change of attitude as soon as they left.

"Julie," said Sabrina, "What happened to your leg? Have you got time for lunch?"

Surprise, surprise.

———

They went to Press 101, right across the parking lot. It was busy, but they were fortunate to grab an outside table on the edge of the crowd where Julie could stow her crutches and prop up her leg.

It was obvious that Sabrina wanted to unburden herself of something, but they eased into it, making small talk until their sandwiches were delivered.

"I have to tell you something that may have a bearing on what happened to Dianna Wieland," said Sabrina. "I don't think it *does*, but I'm glad to have somebody other than the police to discuss it with."

"Of course," said Julie, leaning forward in her best listening pose.

"First of all, you need to know that Mike Menello lives with me, Julie. We've been together ever since he lost his house in that Quill Creek fiasco. Do you know about that? About the lakefront lots he bought there?"

"Yes, I do," said Julie. "I understand that he bought them at the top of the bubble and built two high-end homes."

"Yes, and then the market collapsed and Mike lost everything. You have to *know* Mike to understand what I'm about to say, Julie. He's the kind of man who can't admit having made a mistake and losing. He couldn't let it go. He blamed the seller of the lots and the seller's agent, Bay Street Realty…and more specifically, Dianna Wieland. He really hated her; he accused her of conspiring with the appraiser, too.

"The thing is…the thing that's bothering me is…I'm not a hundred percent *sure* that Mike was at my house the night…or the morning...when Dianna died."

Sabrina ignored her food. Her elbows were on the table, her head forward, her eyes closed.

She pinched the bridge of her nose.

A lot of self conflict. She loves Mike Menello… some kind of predicament.

"What makes you uncertain?"

"I take strong sleeping pills for insomnia and I have a huge bed. The mattress was very expensive; I paid a lot of money so that I wouldn't feel so much as a *ripple* on my side if someone jumped up and down on the other. The truth is that I really wouldn't have known if Mike left for a few hours and came back."

"But why would you suspect him of doing something like that?

"Because he did it *before*," said Sabrina, sighing. "I woke up one night and he was *gone*, Julie. The next morning he said he had a headache and he'd gone out looking for a drugstore that was open; he said he needed Excedrin Migraine, which I didn't have. I believed him…until I thought about it some more."

"Perhaps he *did* go to the drugstore," said Julie.

"No…I'm sure now that he didn't."

Sabrina was running her hand through her hair, unconsciously massaging her head.

The stress is huge…she's trying to relieve it. C'mon, just get it out, Sabrina.

"How can you be sure?"

"Because he left the house in the middle of the night *again*…and I followed him."

"Where did he go?" asked Julie, intrigued.

"To Lake Eola…well, not actually to the lake, although he parked in Eola Park Center."

Sabrina looked up at Julie almost apologetically. Clearly, she knew the significance of that.

"He didn't go to the Lake," said Sabrina. "He went to a restaurant, a *closed restaurant*, the Mint Julep. *Somebody let him in* and I just don't know what to make of it."

"What time was that?"

"It was sometime after one in the morning," said Sabrina.

"When did he come out?"

"He *didn't*. I stayed, driving around like a crazy person, until three. Then I gave it up and went home. I was exhausted but I knew I'd never get to sleep, so I cut one of my pills in half and took it. When I woke up at half-past nine, he was in bed…snoring."

Julie sat quiet for awhile, mulling over this strange turn of events. She thought about Mike Menello, as he'd been described to her by Joe, Lee Porter and Sabrina…and she developed a hypothesis.

"While Mike's behavior is suspicious, Sabrina, and it might put him in the area at the time Dianna died…it *doesn't* necessarily mean that he had anything to do with it. The important thing here is to get to the truth. Now, listen," she said, "I'm going to tell you what I think is happening, and I'm going to ask you to trust me. We need to get you off the hook on the matter of this alibi *without letting Mike know that you followed him or you talked to me*, all right?"

Sabrina leaned forward with rapt attention.

44

~~~

"How long has he been gone?" said Joe Garrett.

"About ten minutes. He left at half-past twelve."

"All right, Sabrina. Thank you for calling me; you're doing the right thing."

"I hope so. You'll let me know what happens?"

"Absolutely. As soon as I can."

"Okay…bye."

"Bye," said Joe, clicking off and immediately dialing another number.

"Ahem…this is McPhee," said the police detective, clearing his throat.

"Hi. It's Joe Garrett. Mike Menello left Nolen's house in Windsor Place ten minutes ago."

"Okay. We'll give him a little time. You want to come along?"

"No, but I appreciate the invite. Merlin and I need to keep a low profile here. Menello knows that we talked to Sabrina before. We don't want him to know that she's the snitch."

"No problem," said McPhee. "I'll keep her name out of it."

"Good, thanks. Bye."

"Thank *you,*" said McPhee.

Joe clicked off and speed-dialed Julie.

"Hello?"

Her voice was soft with sleep, and Joe could picture her curled up in her bed.

"Sorry to wake you, Julie. I wanted to let you know that Sabrina called and it's going down in a half-hour or so."

"Oh, that's good, Joe. I'm glad he finally went out; poor Sabrina hasn't gotten any sleep for a week. When will we know?"

"I suppose McPhee will call me tomorrow sometime."

"Okay…that's good. You must be tired, too. Get some sleep, Joe."

"I will, honey. See you in the morning."

They hung up.

Julie was right; Joe was dead-tired. He could hear his bed calling his name. He'd been staying up late all week waiting for Sabrina's call, afraid he might not hear the phone.

He stood up, and headed for the bedroom, yawning.

Well, it's in McPhee's hands now.

Two days later there was an article in the Orlando
Sentinel Newspaper:

Police Raid Illegal Poker Room
By John Greeley

*Early Wednesday morning, the Orlando
Police Department raided an illegal poker
room in the Mint Julep restaurant in
Downtown Orlando. A source at the OPD
suggested that there were several of these clubs
in the city and that police were going
undercover to bust them all.*

*The club at the Mint Julep was operating
several nights per week from midnight until
four in the morning to avoid detection. The
poker room had sophisticated security in place
to keep uninvited visitors away, but that didn't
stop an undercover police officer from gaining
access and signaling the SWAT team.*

*WESH News was on scene to capture the
bust. Twelve people, all dealers and their
bosses, were taken into custody during the raid
and charged with organized crime. Other
employees and players will be subpoenaed
later and will have to appear in court.*

*There were ten poker tables and over
$30,000 in play seized by the police. It was not
possible to estimate the amount of profit
regularly taken by the operators.*

A player of particular interest to Sabrina Nolen, Joe Garrett and Julie O'Hara – not to mention the Orlando Police – was caught on video exiting the Mint Julep in a hurry.

45

"How did you know, Merlin?" asked Joe. "You never even met the guy."

Julie limped over to her desk. It was her first day without the crutches.

"From listening to people who interacted with him," she said, sitting down. "From Sabrina and Lee Porter, and from what Detective McPhee told you.

"Mike Menello has all the traits of a compulsive gambler. He lives in a dream world. He can't accept reality and he takes risks based on his *dream*. That's what he did when he bought the lots in Quill Creek. He fancied himself a competent contractor, which he wasn't. The subcontractors saw how green he was and they took advantage of it. And, of course, he couldn't accept responsibility for the outcome, so he blamed other people...primarily Dianna.

"He's immature. He feels he's entitled to the good things in life without having to work for them; that's why it doesn't bother him that Sabrina pays the bills and gives him pocket money. And then there's the fact that he kept sneaking out at night to go Downtown to the Lake Eola area, despite the cloud over him because of Dianna's death. Not to mention that Sabrina was *bound* to catch him, sooner or later. I'd say that Mike Menello is anxious to the point of being sick until he sits at a poker table…that's what made him take those risks."

Julie had a pile of work on her desk and she began to sort it out.

"So Sabrina was right," said Joe. "Menello wasn't at her house when Dianna died."

"Well, not the whole night. I'm sure he'll admit to that now," said Julie. "The police have a lot of witnesses under subpoena who can testify as to whether or not he was there."

"It's no alibi for the time of the murder, though," said Joe. "Everyone was leaving the Mint Julep around four that morning, shortly before the time the coroner said Dianna died, which would have been somewhere around five. And if Sabrina didn't wake up until after seven, she can't really say when Menello returned. That's a two-hour window of opportunity."

"That's true, Joe, but at least Sabrina knows *where* he was going and *why*. Believe it or not, I think she loves the guy, warts and all. Besides, even if Mike Menello was in the area, the police don't have any evidence linking him –or anyone else – to her death."

"Well…maybe they do," said Joe, looking away.

"I don't believe it!" she said, slapping a file on her desk. "You're holding out on me! What evidence do they have?"

"I'm not 'holding out' on you, I'm telling you *now*. McPhee just mentioned it the other day when I tipped him about the poker room. I forgot about it."

"So what is it?"

"A very small blood sample that didn't match Dianna's. McPhee said they almost missed it. It was on the neck of the swan boat. OPD couldn't demand blood samples from people with solid alibis who were ruled out as suspects, so they decided to hold it back. But now that Menello's alibi is blown, I'm sure they'll test him."

Julie had resumed sorting her files, but Joe could see the wheels turning in her head.

"Don't get too hopeful about this, Merlin. The sample might be worthless. It could have been from any number of visitors who rented the swan the day before."

She stopped what she doing and looked squarely at him.

"Or it *could* belong to Dianna's killer…"

46

Sabrina and John Tate, Mike's attorney, were finally able to convince him that he needed to preempt a possible arrest by going, posthaste, to the Orlando Police Department and coming clean about his whereabouts the morning of Dianna Wieland's death. Although Mike had apologized profusely to Sabrina for lying to her and had even acknowledged his gambling addiction, he was very indignant that anyone should suspect him of *murder*.

After calling Detective McPhee to advise him that his client was coming in, John Tate immediately escorted Mike to police headquarters. A thorough interrogation ensued and Mike was asked to give a blood and DNA sample. On his attorney's advice, he complied and was then released, pending the results.

Given Mike's penchant for lying, John Tate was preparing for the worst and Sabrina was on pins and needles. The only one who wasn't worried about the outcome of the test was Mike.

—

At roughly the same time, Dianna's killer was thinking about Mike, too. He was watching a WESH 2 news follow-up report on TV…

   "*Michael Menello of Orlando, who was recently involved in the raid of an illegal poker room near Lake Eola, is now being called "a person of interest" in the death of real estate agent, Dianna Wieland, whose body was discovered at Lake Eola this past January.*"

   This development was bad news and good news all at once, he thought. It meant that they no longer thought of Dianna's death as a suicide…but it also meant that Menello, who fed them a phony alibi, was their number one suspect.
   Somebody else might have felt bad about that, but not him.
   Shit happens…
   If anyone knows that, I do.

47

Joe and Julie were on their way to see Betty Wieland. It was incumbent upon them to let her know about Hoyt Geller's death and to return the shoebox of his letters. Betty had been standing up to her domineering husband at every opportunity since Dianna's death, and Frank had loosened his grip on her as a result. Isolated and rebuffed, Frank Wieland had succumbed to the invitation of a neighbor to try his hand at golf. He was not expected to return for at least two hours.

"I'm glad the police have a suspect," said Joe. He was turning into the Wieland's neighborhood and he lowered his window to give his name to the guard at the subdivision's gate. Once they were waved through, he continued. "The Wielands will be encouraged to see that OPD is still pursuing the case and not dismissing it as a suicide."

"I know they will, Joe, but I strongly suspect that Mike Menello is *not* the killer."

"I don't think so, either, Julie. Menello is a dandy, from what I hear. I can't picture his type lurking around with a switchblade. And he would have been tired at four in the morning and looking to get back before Sabrina woke up."

"My thoughts exactly. Also, how would he have known Dianna was there?" said Julie. "Obviously, he wasn't following her around. He was obsessed with *poker*, not Dianna."

They pulled into the Wieland's driveway and got out of the Land Rover.

"Let's try to ease into this news, Joe. It's going to hit her hard. She already feels guilty about Hoyt going to prison and what he endured there. To learn that the Gellers died so tragically not long after he was released…."

Joe nodded.

The door opened before they got to it.

"Hi," said Betty. "I was watching for you. Come on in."

She led them to the dining room, where there was a pot of coffee and brownies. Julie was glad to see that Betty's demeanor was a little less haunted.

She's coping much better, glad to see us.

"It's early, so I thought we'd have some coffee," she said as Julie and Joe sat down at the table. "Why don't I take that box from you? I'll put it back in the garage while you two help yourselves, all right?"

Joe handed her the box.

"Thanks," said Betty. "Be careful. It's a thermal pot; it really keeps the coffee hot."

Julie took it upon herself to pour them each a cup of coffee and Joe, who loved chocolate, happily took two brownies. In a couple of minutes, Betty was back.

She poured a cup for herself.

"I see that the police are making some progress on the case," she said. "The paper said that Michael Menello filed a complaint against Bay Street Realty last year…something about a land deal he made. He *threatened* Dianna."

"Yes, he did do that," said Joe. "He was upset because he lost a lot of money, but it wasn't the agency's fault, Betty."

"Oh, I knew that. Kate and Dianna would never cheat anyone. Why, everybody has lost property value in this recession! That man probably has mental problems."

"He does have a problem, Betty, but I don't know if it's relevant," said Joe. "He's a compulsive gambler."

"I saw that!" she said. "He got caught in the raid on that restaurant right near where Dianna died! I'd say that's 'relevant'. "

Julie thought it was time to come to Joe's aid.

"I think what Joe means is that, while the location of the restaurant is certainly of interest, Mike Menello's gambling addiction actually makes it *less* likely that he followed Dianna and attacked her, Betty. We think that he was obsessed with poker, not revenge."

"Then why are the police calling him 'a person of interest'?'

"Because he was near the scene and he concocted a false alibi to hide the fact. They *will* charge him, though, if they think they have enough evidence," said Joe.

"But you don't think he's the one," said Betty, crestfallen.

"No," said Julie. "But we have conclusively ruled out suicide, Betty."

Tears welled in her eyes and she grabbed Julie's hand.

"Who else could it have been, then…Hoyt?" She looked from Joe to Julie. "Hoyt went *crazy* in prison! He might have blamed Dianna, followed her here!"

"No, he didn't, Betty," said Julie, as gently as possible. "Hoyt Geller is dead. He died in Massachusetts in 2006. It was a truck accident; his parents died, too." Julie reached into her purse and withdrew a copy of the newspaper article and gave it to her.

"Oh, no," she said, reading it, pressing a tissue to her lips. "They just got him back after seven years."

Betty covered her face with her hands and cried.

Julie silently put her arm around her, and Joe lowered his eyes to the table cloth.

"Hoyt was such a handsome boy," Betty said. "It was no wonder Dianna loved him. He looked like that actor in the movies who died young, too." She sniffed, collecting herself. "You know that movie with Sal Mineo? Oh, I forgot. You're too young…you wouldn't remember him."

But Julie was a fan of old movies and she already knew where this was leading.

"Do you mean 'Rebel Without A Cause'?"

"That's the one. Natalie Wood was in it, too. Hoyt looked like the other actor…what was his name?"

"James Dean," said Julie.

"Yes…spitting image."

They had just gotten into the Land Rover outside the house.

"It's Lincoln Tyler," said Joe, pulling out of the driveway, "he's Hoyt Geller!"

"Has to be…*can't* be a coincidence," said Julie. "That's why Dianna was so interested in him. Remember what Sabrina Nolen said about Dianna at the Rodeo, 'she almost fell over the railing trying to talk to him' or something like that? Dianna knew it was Hoyt!"

"We've got to tell McPhee," said Joe.

"What? Tell him *what*, Joe? That Linc looks like James Dean? That a guy who died in Massachusetts in 2006 also looked like James Dean? And we're basing this on the memory of a woman who last saw the one in Massachusetts fourteen years ago?"

"Well…we can explain it better than that…"

"No, we can't, Joe. I've got to go see Lincoln. I couldn't read him accurately before; he was too accomplished at the James Dean impersonation and we didn't know enough about him. He won't be able to fool me now. I'll get the truth, about what happened in Massachusetts…and about Dianna."

Joe knew Julie too well to think he could stop her now.

"Well, you're sure as hell not going to be alone with him! I'm going with you."

48

The drive to Ocala seemed to take forever. Maybe that was because their investigation, to this point, had taken so long and now they were anticipating a breakthrough. Julie had joined forces with Joe in March and it was almost the end of May. On the plus side, her leg was getting stronger. The physical therapist had just given her a thumbs-up on a daily walk. "No running, though," he'd warned. "You'll break it again!"

Julie looked up, out the window of the Land Rover. The summer weather pattern seemed to be starting early this year. There hadn't been a cloud in the sky this morning when they went to the Wielands' house, but now they were drifting in, here and there, and a thunderstorm was predicted for the late afternoon.

"Linc's not happy about this third visit," said Joe, turning onto the now familiar, two-lane road leading to Pleasure Ride Ranch.

"What did he say?"

"That he was working with three horses and he was 'really busy'. He said he didn't know when he 'could get around' to us. I told him it wasn't a problem; we'd wait all day if necessary."

"I hope we don't have to wait all day. I think we're in for a storm," said Julie.

"You watch, Merlin, he'll see us right away. That was just a stall. He couldn't put me off, so he'll want to get it over with and get rid of us."

Joe turned in under the green and black arch with the *PR* brand circled in the center. The ranch was the same: the long red clay drive bordered by corral fencing, horses grazing on lush lawns and tall oaks strung with moss, the white ranch buildings trimmed in black and green. And yet, it seemed different. Julie decided that it was the increasing cloudiness of the sky, and perhaps the time of day, too.

The first time I saw Pleasure Ride it was late afternoon, the slanting sun had striped the ranch in golden tones. It's still beautiful, but the glowing, storybook effect is gone…

Julie spotted Lincoln Tyler and another man in a big oval corral down a short path to the right of the main house.

"There's Lincoln over there, Joe."

"I better park here; that path isn't made for cars. Can you walk that far?"

"Oh, sure. The exercise is good for my leg. My therapist wants me to walk."

Fortunately, the wide path was firm and relatively even.

Lincoln saw them coming, took off his Stetson and waved it. He said a few words to the other fellow, slapped his hat on his jeans and put it back on. He started across the corral towards them.

"What did I tell you?" said Joe in an aside. "No wait."

"Hey, there, Mr. Garrett, Ms. O'Hara. Welcome back," drawled Lincoln.

He's planning to do James Dean for this whole meeting.

I don't think so, Lincoln…

"Hi, Linc," said Joe.

"Hello, Lincoln," said Julie." "Or should we call you Hoyt?"

Julie watched carefully as the shock totally took him out of the James Dean persona. There was no doubt that Hoyt Geller was the man standing before them. It didn't take an expert to see it. Julie was sure that Joe saw it, too.

It's almost like Multiple Personality Disorder, except he's fully aware of it. Hoyt Geller is a third person…an entirely different person, distinct from the roles of James Dean and Lincoln Tyler. Even his posture has changed.

"Call me Lincoln. I think we need to talk this over in my cottage."

"Sure," said Joe, opening his jacket just enough to let him see his shoulder holster.

Lincoln got the message.

"You don't have to worry about me, Mr. Garrett. I'm the one who needs to be worried here. Let's go."

Julie and Joe followed him to the simple white cottage where he lived. They climbed the two wide plank stairs out front, passing by three white rockers aligned on the porch in front of the windows. It was clouding up and looked like it might rain...or maybe Lincoln felt this was an indoor kind of conversation.

He hit a wall switch and a couple of table lamps came on, glowing softly against the Florida knotty pine walls and rafters. Julie noticed cowboy art hung here and there. Considering the steep green metal roof outside, she shouldn't have been surprised to see that the small building's only bedroom was upstairs in an open loft, but she was. The first floor was all one large room. A small kitchen was tucked away in the corner with a round table and four chairs. Sitting on a wide area rug in front of a charred stone fireplace were a serviceable old couch and two chairs.

Lincoln tossed his Stetson onto one side of a handsome set of longhorns mounted on the fireplace and plopped in one of the chairs.

"Have a seat," he said. "This is probably going to take awhile. How'd you find out?"

"Dianna's mother suffered terrible guilt about the conviction of Hoyt Geller," said Julie. "She never agreed with her husband that Hoyt had taken advantage of Dianna. Our research turned up the fact that Hoyt and his family died in an accident on their farm. We showed a newspaper article about it to Betty Wieland this morning. She cried over the death of "poor Hoyt and his parents". And guess what, Lincoln? She mentioned that poor Hoyt looked '*just like James Dean*'.

"We could have called the police immediately," said Julie. "But we decided to ask you some questions, to get your explanation first. So let's get a big one out of the way. I'm guessing that the real Lincoln Tyler died in the crash with your parents. Do you want to tell us exactly how that 'accident' happened and who he was?"

Linc took a deep breath and slowly let it out. It was a sigh worthy of Atlas shrugging off the weight of the world.

"You're right. Lincoln Tyler was my friend, kind of like a brother. He was born in Maine and left at an orphanage. He never knew his real parents. He ran away from an abusive foster home when he was sixteen and ended up in Massachusetts. He was living in a cabin in our town, barely getting by. Meanwhile, my parents had lost more than a son when I went to prison, they'd lost a farmhand, too. They hired Lincoln to help out.. He was only two years younger than me and he took my place in more ways than one.

"But you have to understand; I was *glad* about that. Prison changed me...I didn't want to live at home anymore, you know? Having Lincoln there made it easier for me to leave, at least I thought it would.

"It turned out that, Lincoln or no Lincoln, *leaving* was impossible. First of all, I couldn't get a job. Every employment application asked, 'Have you ever been convicted of a crime?' If I said 'yes', they wanted all the details and I didn't get the job. So, I lied…and I got a job…and then I got fired when they found out I lied.

"I didn't give up easily, though. I started looking for jobs that didn't require applications…and I found one…a landscaping company. It was going all right until the police came and dragged me out the house, grilled me and threw me in a line-up. A three year-old girl was missing from the next town and they thought I had something to do with it.

"*A three year-old.*

"I was registered as a *Sex Offender* for the crime of falling in love with Dianna Wieland, a full grown girl, with whom I'd never had sex. I'm sorry if I sound angry. This is something I've tried hard not to think about. Shall I continue?"

"Yes," said Julie, understanding his anger. "Please go on."

She'd been watching Linc's every expression, every nuance, and there wasn't one false note.

Overall, he was relaxed and his body was still. His rate of blinking and the pitch of his voice were normal; his gaze was steady. There were no hesitations, no 'ums' and 'ahs'. Most of all, up to this point, his story rang true and didn't contradict what they already knew.

"The newspaper picked up the story and I lost my job, so I came to the decision that there was no point in leaving the farm," he said. "I had the love and support of my parents, who knew the truth about me. I had a good friend in Lincoln, who had also lived through some tough times. I even had a girlfriend who wasn't too picky about the company she kept.

"Anyway, our farm had extensive apple orchards and other stuff going on…it was sort of a local attraction…especially in the fall. I would eventually inherit the place and it was a decent, dependable business. It was a hell of a lot better than prison…and it was better than moving somewhere and having to *register* as a perpetual scumbag suspect."

"So how did the accident happen?" asked Joe. His tone made two things plain: he was impatient and unconvinced.

"It was spring, April. That's when we check the fencing around our property. Some of it is just wood and chicken wire, but up on the ridge, way in the back of our land, we have chain link for safety. There's a granite quarry right behind us there, and the land drops off sharply. My father was driving our old pickup truck; my mother was in the cab beside him. It was a nice day; she brought our lunch and came along for the ride. Lincoln and I were in the back with the tools.

"It all happened so fast, and I don't really know how. We were next to the fence…"

Julie noticed that Linc's pattern of speech had unconsciously slowed and the pitch of his voice was lower, both signs of extreme sadness. Tears were glistening in his eyes. He closed them momentarily and continued.

"My father was supposed to back up...but he didn't. He stepped on the gas. He had to have stepped on the pedal *hard*...but he couldn't have meant to do it.

"We shot forward through the fence and I was thrown clear before the truck hit. The fire swept through right away...everyone was...they were all..."

Linc stood up, unable to go on. He stood in the kitchen, his back to Julie and Joe, rocking back and forth, his arms crossed, his fist to his mouth. Joe looked at Julie and he was choked up, too. It was utterly impossible to doubt the truth of Linc's account.

After a couple minutes, he returned to his chair.

"I'm sorry. Anyway, that's it. That's what happened. I should have died with them, but Lincoln Tyler did. So now what?"

Neither one of them could move on without expressing their sympathy.

"I'm sorry about your parents, Linc," said Julie.

"Yeah," said Joe. "I'm sorry, man."

"Thank you. What else do you want to know?"

Joe had to know one thing.

"Why did you move to Florida? Was it Dianna?"

"Yes," admitted Linc. "I felt like she was all I had left. I found out where she lived, but I was afraid to contact her. I didn't know how she felt about me. What if she hated me like her father? I was building a new life here at the ranch, one where I wasn't a social outcast. She could blow it apart.

"Two years went by, but I kept thinking of her. Finally, I decided to take a limited chance."

He got up and took a picture off the wall.

"I sent her a copy of this, with a note on it that said, 'I'll be there again this year'. I signed it Linc Tyler."

It was a framed Silver Spurs Rodeo photograph of Linc on horseback hoisting a trophy. His smiling face was clearly visible.

"She recognized you and she came," said Joe.

"Yes, she came."

"What happened after that?" said Joe.

"Everything was wonderful after that. I didn't care about anything that had gone on before, none of it mattered. You have to understand; Dianna was everything I ever wanted, since I was sixteen. It was the happiest time of my life."

"Were you angry when she broke it off?"

"Yes, I was. Very."

I think we've heard enough. One last question…

"Did you kill Dianna, Linc?" asked Julie.

"No. Of course not, I loved her! I came to my senses. There was no realistic basis for *us*. What was she going to do, bring me home to meet her parents? Marry a sexual predator, her very *own* sexual predator, a man hiding out in a false identity? No. Dianna was educated and successful; she had all the makings of a good life ahead of her. *There was no way for us to be together*. I forced myself to accept the facts.

"Later, when I heard about her death, I was stunned. My best friends, grief and fear were back in spades. And *rage*. I knew Dianna didn't kill herself and there was *nothing* I could do! Then that detective, McPhee, and his partner came to see me. What if they found out who I was? And then *you* showed up. I really got scared when you went to Folsom, the trainer in Palm Meadows. Oh, yeah, he called me. He's a good guy, but he told me he really didn't see me out at the track that morning.

"When I hung up from him, I thought for sure the cops were going to dig deeper and end up hanging Dianna's death on me. I had to find some *other* way to verify where I was. The hotel was out. I left the Best Western about six to go watch Beau Grande run, but I didn't stop at the desk. I got gas later, too, but I threw away the slip. And then I thought of this…"

Linc opened up the drawer of the end table next to him and handed Julie a sheet of paper.

"It's my credit union statement. Look at January 28, 2010. Right under the Best Western, Boynton Beach, there's another debit, Champion Stop & Go, Boynton Beach.

"Well, now you know the whole story. Dianna loved me in a way, but not like I loved her. We had our time together because we had paid a heavy price for it. We *deserved* it. It was as simple as that."

The windshield wipers drummed a steady beat and the headlights of the Land Rover cut through the driving rain. They were quiet; no need to state the obvious.

"So, now what do we do?"

"I don't know, Joe. I don't know."

There was *one* thing they both knew:

They would keep Linc Tyler's secret.

49

It was July and hot as hell. Fortunately, Mother Nature gathered her thunderclouds most afternoons and thoroughly doused a grateful Florida. Suburbanites in Orlando threw open their garage doors welcoming the cool air and, while sipping iced-tea, enjoyed the booming light show and deluge from beach chairs inside.

Downtown, Julie and Joe watched the downpour through the screen door of Joe's kitchen. The rain was coming straight down and the second-floor porch roof – designed precisely for such an occasion – was keeping the small outside deck dry. Nevertheless, they had covered the grill and moved their meal inside.

Two months had passed since they had gone to Pleasure Ride Farm in Ocala. Joe had officially wrapped up his investigation and sent a full report to the Wielands and a copy to Detective McPhee at the Orlando Police Department. Julie, however, could not let the case go. Once again, she had brought up the subject…and Joe was losing patience.

"Look, we did lift some guilt from the Wielands, and the cops have to keep the case open. And another thing, it certainly eased Sabrina's mind when Mike was cleared with the DNA test. That wouldn't have happened without us. Sabrina would never have gone directly to the cops."

"Yeah, I guess," said Julie, patently unsatisfied.

"Do you know how many murder cases go unsolved, Merlin? No? Well, let me tell you; it's *one out of three*. We did the best we could, so stop beating yourself up! Isn't it enough that you got your leg broken?"

Julie sipped her chardonnay and kept quiet.

No, it isn't. It feels like I got my leg broken for nothing.

"By the way," said Joe, "how *is* your leg?"

"It's better. I managed to climb the stairs without any problem. I'm glad to be off the crutches. At least I can do some simple things, like cooking. How's your tortellini?" Julie had made one of her favorite dishes: tortellini with fresh vegetables, parmesan cheese and chicken.

"Magnifico," said Joe, raising his wine glass.

He was right, of course. She had to let go of Dianna's case, put it out of her mind. She raised her glass to his.

"You know, Joe, we're a couple of *foodies*."

"Yes, we are," he agreed, smiling. "It's one of the things we do really well."

She just couldn't help herself.

Unlike solving murders…

50

Dianna's killer was feeling good. He was dressed for summer in black shorts, sneakers and a green shirt. It was a nice day to be out riding on the bike. He was nodding and smiling at people and they were smiling back at him. He particularly liked looking at the girls with their short-shorts and skimpy tops. He tipped his cap at one of them.

That's the good thing about these sunglasses. They can't see what I'm looking at.

He laughed to himself.

He was sorry about what happened to Dianna, but it was *her* fault, treating him like that. Did she think he was just going to take it?

Besides, it was months ago now. He began to whistle.

Life was good…

51

It was the hour that didn't make sense to Julie.

If Dianna died between five-thirty and six o'clock in the morning, her killer had to be out there hanging around Lake Eola at five or earlier...before dawn.

Julie had great respect for gut instinct. Sometimes over-thinking a problem led to erroneous conclusions. In the very beginning, when everyone thought Dianna's death was a suicide, part of that conclusion was born of gut instinct. Joe had voiced it well: "What mugger, or rapist, or whatever, would even be *awake*?"

The answer was *none*. It was common knowledge that the area was largely deserted at that time of the morning. In fact, that was why the poker club patrons at the Mint Julep could exit unobserved at that hour. Even the craziest drug addict, rapist or thief wouldn't hang around a typically deserted area hoping for a mark to materialize on foot.

Dianna's death wasn't a suicide and it wasn't random, Julie decided. She was targeted by someone who knew exactly where she was. This was someone waiting patiently - most likely in a vehicle - for Dianna, specifically, to materialize. And it wasn't Lee Porter, Mike Menello or Lincoln Tyler. That left only one possibility.

Dianna had a stalker.

That meant that her death was about sex and obsession. It meant that someone fantasized a relationship with Dianna that didn't exist.

Suddenly, Julie had an idea. She picked up the phone and keyed in number.

"Tate Law Firm...Good morning."

"Hi, is this Carol?" said Julie.

"Yes, it is. How can I help you?"

"It's Merlin, Carol. I'm calling for John. Is he in?"

"Just a moment, Merlin. I'll see…"

John Tate came on the line.

"Merlin! How are you? Are you available? I've got an important case. I'm going to need some assistance with jury selection."

"I'm fine. When?" said Julie.

"Two weeks from Monday."

"I can't see why not, John. I'll check my calendar with Luz and get back to you on that later today, all right? But, right now, I need a referral."

"Sure, what kind?"

"I need the name of an expert on stalkers and rapists."

"Are you and Joe still investigating Dianna Wieland's death?"

"Not officially and not the two of us. Joe has already made his report to the Wielands. However, I'm not personally ready to let Dianna's case go. I'm convinced that she had a stalker, John. I need a better understanding of this sort of person. Do you know an expert?"

"Yes. I'd recommend Lyle Jordan. He's a Forensic Psychologist that I've used a couple times in the past. He's brilliant."

52

Julie arrived early for her four-thirty appointment with Dr. Lyle Jordan, sensitive to the fact that he was squeezing her in at the end of his day. She'd had no difficulty locating Dr. Jordan's tucked-away house with her phone's GPS directions. The home was a two-story Victorian in Windermere, a unique little enclave sandwiched by the pristine lakes of the Butler chain. The man's office was an afterthought, an attached one-floor wing.

Julie rang the bell and Jordan himself came to the door to let her in. He was a senior, graying and somewhat stooped. He wore a white shirt; open at the collar, its short sleeves exposing forearms covered with age spots. There was a faint odor escaping on his breath that caused Julie to wonder if he might be ill.

She gave him her card and followed him through a small anteroom into his private office. Dr. Jordan pulled out the comfortable leather chair that bore his outline, and sat behind his desk. All four walls were lined with books and various degrees and certification. Two of them had windows with woodland views. It was a warm room for a studious occupant. He motioned for her to take a chair.

"So you have an interest in stalkers, I understand, Ms. O'Hara."

Julie presumed that John had given Lyle Jordan that information.

"Yes. In connection with a death, Dr. Jordan. Do you recall the case of Dianna Wieland, whose body was found several months ago at Lake Eola Park?"

"Yes, indeed. The swan boat," he said. "So intriguing! Like the madrigal by Orlando Gibbons. Do you know it?"

Julie shook her head. She had no idea what he was talking about.

"No, I'm afraid not."

"Hold on," he said, standing. He turned and removed a book from the case behind him and began flipping through it. "Yes. Here it is. *The Silver Swan…*

> *'The silver swan,*
> *who living had no Note,*
> *When Death approached*
> *unlocked her silent throat.'*

"I don't know what made me think of it. But it seems apropos, doesn't it?" he said.

"Very."

"Yes. Well, then," said Dr. Jordan, replacing the book. "John Tate told me that you've been working on an investigative team for the victim's parents. How can I assist you?"

Julie decided that it would be unproductive to mention that the investigation was closed and she was no longer part of a team.

"It seems unlikely, Doctor, that Dianna Wieland committed suicide. It is also unlikely, in my opinion, that her death was a random crime. That leads me to believe that she may have had a stalker. I hoped you could help me develop a profile of such a person, Dr. Jordan."

"Well, first, I would have to say that you are going to need more information, Ms. O'Hara. That is much easier to come by when you have a *live* victim, of course. There are five broad categories of stalkers, you see."

Julie pulled out a notebook and a pen.

"Can you describe them, briefly?"

"All right," he said, thoughtfully, leaning back in his chair. "Of course, stalkers are male and female, both young and old. It's all about obsession. Usually, their behavior gets worse over time. Stalking can be triggered by anger, sex, power or merely a desire for intimacy with the victim. It can range from repeated phone calls to extreme violence.

"When you don't have input from the victim, you have to examine very carefully all the rest of the available information. So, let's proceed by elimination,

Ms. O'Hara," he said, leaning forward, "keeping in mind, of course, that this is *conjecture*."

"Of course," said Julie

"I think we're probably safe to assume that the stalker here would be a male, since the victim was female. A question: Have all the men in her life been examined…including prior relationships?"

"Yes," said Julie. "They've all been cleared."

"All right. That type, as you may have guessed, is known as the Rejected Suitor, a man who can't take it when a relationship ends. Another type I think we can rule out is the Intimacy Seeker. They are generally delusional and looking for love.

"The Incompetent Suitor is also not as prone to violence. He's a man who has asked a woman out on a date and been rejected. His main goal is to change a woman's mind through persistent stalking ¬behavior which he thinks of as 'courting'.

"I would say that the most likely candidate would be one of these two:

"The very dangerous one that you see in the movies, the Predatory Stalker, is actually not as common as people think. This is a man who picks a random woman, gathers information and carefully plans a sexual attack on her. He's likely to be a repeat offender and will kill his victim to cover his crime.

"The other one would be the Resentful Stalker. This one is angry. He's been humiliated by his victim, although *she* may not have perceived it that way. In the beginning - unaware of his obsession problem – his victim may have been nice to him. But when he inevitably becomes intrusive, she puts her foot down. Suddenly, in *his* eyes, *he* becomes a victim. He's looking for power and control over the woman who caused him to feel that way, usually by rape."

He stole a quick look at his watch, but continued politely.

"Something I can't stress enough, Ms. O'Hara: These are very *general* classifications and not everyone agrees with my opinions on them. You must also take into consideration that we are talking about mentally ill people. Stalking behavior escalates and *any* of them are capable of murder under certain circumstances."

"I understand, Dr. Jordan," said Julie, sensing the man's exhaustion. She put away her notes and stood. "It was so nice of you to take the time to explain this complicated subject to me. I can't thank you enough. You've been very helpful."

"Not at all. It was a pleasure to meet you," he said, as he escorted her to the door. "I wish you success in your investigation. If you need anything more, please call me."

Julie had a much clearer picture of Dianna's killer in mind and a plan to find him.

She tossed her zippered purse into her Volkswagen and then sat, back first, in the driver's seat. She eased her healing left leg in last.

Look out, you sick son-of-a-bitch.

I'm coming...

53

~~~

Julie carried a small digital recorder in her purse and, as usual, she had been speaking into it as she drove back to the office, recording the highlights of her meeting with the forensic psychologist. She was nearly done with her recap, as she reached the Downtown area.

"Whoever killed Dianna was unpracticed and clumsy. Otherwise, she wouldn't have ended up with the knife. That doesn't fit the profile of the 'Predatory Stalker' as described by Dr. Jordan. The most likely fit for this suspect is the 'Resentful Stalker', the one who felt 'humiliated'."

She hit the 'pause' button and thought for a moment.

Humiliated…who had Dianna humiliated?

She hit "record".

"Dr. Jordan said that, in the beginning, she 'may have been nice to him, *unaware* of his obsession.' So, at some point, Dianna realized what she was dealing with, and she 'put her foot down'. She pissed him off…maybe embarrassed him. She didn't think it was a big deal…but *he* did. *That's* the man I'm looking for."

Julie shut off the recorder and dropped it back in her purse as she pulled into the bricked parking area in front of her office.

Luz was at her desk typing something on the computer when Julie walked in. She turned and smiled.

"Hi! You had a few calls, Julie. I put them on your desk."

"Okay, Luz. Thank you," said Julie, hurrying into her office. She was eager to go over the notes of her interviews in Dianna's file - an elusive memory of something there - but first, she addressed the three pink call slips.

Sue Chenoweth, her editor.

I'll call her later. She'll be happy to know that I've almost finished the rewrite.

Attorney John Tate.

I've got to call him, too. Glad there's a couple weeks before that jury gets impaneled.

Joe: "Gone to catch bugs with Will for a couple days. Call you when I get back."

Julie sat down at her desk, amused. She felt a bit envious, too. Joe had gone to Miami to visit his friend, Will Sawyer, who had a twenty-six foot Newton boat. Will and his buddies were going to the Keys for their annual lobster dive. Last year, Julie had enjoyed hanging out with Carolyn Sawyer and the other women, and their elaborate lobster cook-out on the beach.

It's my own fault he didn't invite me…

In order to cover her continued investigation of Dianna's death, Julie had told Joe that she was "swamped" with work, that she "wouldn't have any free time until August".

Joe would have been insulted and upset that she was continuing the investigation on her own. He would have rightly called her 'obsessed'.

Julie reached for Dianna's file in the straw basket on her desk.

Maybe it takes one to catch one…

She lifted it out and began to read the notes, regretting that she didn't have Luz type them. The digital recorder plugged directly into her computer and a software program printed them out. The only problem was that her notes came out in a stream, frequently without punctuation, which made them hard to read.

No matter, it's in here somewhere. What the hell was it?

Julie skipped the parents' initial interview. As an adult, Dianna had kept the Wielands in the dark about her life. Her background with Lincoln Tyler only eliminated him as a suspect. There was nothing there that pointed to her killer.

Evelyn Hoag was a different matter, and Julie went over every bit of that material from the first meeting in Porter's office to the second one at her own condo. Although she was unable to find anything specific in her notes, Julie was convinced that Evelyn might know more.

I'll meet with her again.

Sabrina Nolen and Barry Costello. Julie scanned their interviews quickly.

There's nothing with Sabrina. I think she and Dianna were on the outs, probably over Mike Menello. They weren't seeing much of each other. But Barry? If I can specifically jog his memory, he may remember somebody at the YMCA paying extra attention to Dianna. That makes sense; a stalker could have joined in the activities over there.

Kate Winslow. This was a very rich interview. Julie reread it, word-for-word, correcting the missing punctuation in her head:

"Kate was 'burned' by two experienced agents."

Irrelevant. Doesn't relate to Dianna.

"Dianna went to UCF, was a Business Admin major. She was a partner for five years…"

Too long out of college to have met a stalker there.

"Kate called Mike Menello a natural-born liar."

True, but he didn't stalk and kill Dianna.

"She said that Dianna was in love, 'over the moon'."

Right…with Lee Porter…who didn't kill her, either.

"Kate kidded Dianna about her pal, Hal, but she was teasing."

Wait a minute…back up.

Hal?

Julie's heart beat quickened. There it was... the elusive note she had made that had stuck in the back of her mind. She had asked if Dianna's clients, apart from Menello, were happy. Kate had replied that they were, that "one fellow was too happy. He took up Dianna's time for two weekends before she realized that he couldn't afford a garage".

"Too" happy. A man looking at houses by himself. A man who can't afford a house.

A man named Hal.

Julie grabbed Bay Street Realty's brochure and began dialing.

54

~~~

"Who was that, again?" asked Kate Winslow.

They were sitting at a teak mini-conference table in Kate's spacious inner office at Bay Street Realty. Out of habit, she had directed Julie to a seat facing the windows which looked out on a small pond filled with reeds and backed with pines. A blue heron stood motionless in the shallows unseen by Kate, who sat with her back to the lovely, unspoiled view.

She was frowning, clearly puzzled.

"I don't understand, Julie. This was a client of Dianna's?"

"Not exactly," said Julie. "You called him 'Hal'. I believe you said, 'her pal, Hal'."

"Oh, *him*. Of course. I did mention him, didn't I? What about him?"

"Do you know his last name?"

"No," she said, shaking her head. "Dianna wouldn't have kept it, either. As I said, he wasn't a good prospect. He couldn't qualify for a mortgage."

"Why was that? Bad credit? Do you know what kind of work he did?"

"Gee, I'm sorry. I really don't know much of anything about the guy." She looked at Julie, her eyes widening in sudden comprehension. "You think he had something to do with Dianna's death, don't you?"

"Yes, I do. I think Hal was a stalker. Intentionally or not, I think he killed her."

"Oh, *my God*! If only I knew his last name! We could research the mortgage app! Damn it!" she said. She closed her eyes and leaned forward, her head in her hands. "His legal name probably isn't even 'Hal…maybe it's Harold, or something."

"Yeah. I thought of that, too," said Julie. "Look…it's a starting point, Kate. Can you describe him?"

"Yes! He was blond…a light, natural blond, with a tan. Like you think of Scandinavian people, with sun-bleached eyebrows and blue eyes. Not exactly good looking, but very outdoorsy and healthy looking. Medium height…no, maybe a little shorter than that. He wasn't much taller than Dianna…but she was tall, like you."

"How old was he?"

"Mid-thirties, I'd say. No more than that. He told her he was getting married, I believe. He said that was why he was looking for a house. In fact, that was the reason Dianna dropped him. She said he didn't qualify on his own and he wouldn't bring in his girlfriend."

"She never mentioned what he did for a living?"

"No. Not that I can remember. Do you think there's any chance of finding him?"

"I don't know. But, from what you've said, I'm even more convinced that he's our man."

Kate walked Julie all the way out to her car and hugged her.

"Thank you for what you're doing. Be careful, Julie."

"I will. If I get more information about this guy, Hal, or even confirmation that someone else saw him around Dianna, I'm going to turn it all over to Joe Garrett. He's a damn good detective, Kate. He'll find the guy."

Julie pulled out of the parking lot, glancing at her watch. It was late afternoon, almost five o'clock. Realizing that she wasn't far from the YMCA, she decided to drop by to see if Barry Costello, "trainer to the stars", was there.

Wouldn't the ladies of Dr. Phillips be getting out of work and heading to the gym?

55

Sure enough, when Julie walked into the Y, Barry Costello was sitting behind the desk. A middle-aged, bespectacled woman - who looked more like a librarian - was standing there and welcomed Julie as she approached the desk.

"Hi…can I help you?"

Barry looked up just then.

"I just came in to see Barry."

"Oh, hi, Ms. O'Hara," said Barry, getting up and coming around the desk.

"I just wanted to ask a quick question, Barry. Do you have a minute?"

"Yeah, sure. Let's sit over here."

He led the way to a nearby folding table covered with pamphlets. It was set up under a bulletin board full of information. They pulled out the PVC chairs and sat down.

"Barry, I know you see a lot of people here, but I'm wondering if you might remember a man who may have been in an exercise class with Dianna Wieland or known her, somehow, from here at the Y."

"Whoever it is, he wouldn't be from her exercise class, Ms. O'Hara. They're all women."

"Oh, okay. Well, maybe you've seen him anyway. He's light blond, maybe Scandinavian, blue eyes, early thirties, not too tall. Sound like anyone you've seen working out here, or on any kind of athletic team here?"

Barry thought about it for a minute.

"There's a guy that plays basketball that's really blond like that, but I don't think he's that old and he's at least six-feet tall…maybe more. He's the only one I can think of."

"Do you know his name?"

"Um…Darren, Daryl…starts with a "D"…*Derek*. It's Derek."

Julie sighed. "I don't think that's him, but thanks anyway, Barry."

"Sure, no problem."

They went back toward the desk, where the librarian-type woman looked at Julie guiltily and said, "I didn't mean to eavesdrop, but I think I've seen the man you're looking for."

"You have?"

"Yes, I think so. It was quite a while back, towards the end of last year. But a man fitting that description – except he wasn't really pale like Derek – anyway, he came in asking for Dianna Wieland. He thought she worked here. I told him she was just a volunteer."

"Did he ask where she worked?"

The woman bit her lip and put her hand to her mouth.

Julie didn't need an answer.

       ——

Getting out of her car in the garage under her condo building, Julie felt a familiar dread. It reminded her of the basement stairs in her childhood home in Boston. There was no light switch at the top of the stone staircase in the old house…which meant that you went down, and climbed up again later, in darkness.

I always ran up those stairs in fear of what might be lurking behind me…even though I'd just turned out the light and knew the cellar was empty.

It wasn't quite dark yet, and all corners of the condo garage were clearly visible. It was as devoid of monsters as her cellar had always been, yet Julie nearly ran to the elevator, her heart slowing only when the doors were fully closed.

There's a difference. The monster has been here.

The feeling, albeit lessened, resurfaced as she stepped out of the elevator on her floor and quickly entered her code into the new lock on her door.

Julie stepped into the safety of her condo and Sol came loping out of the bedroom to greet her. To her delight, everything was shipshape, the cat having slept away the day. She kicked off her shoes, dropped her purse on the wall table by the door and bent over to hug the big cat.

"So…how was *your* day, Handsome? Slept through it, huh? Want to go out?"

She opened the French doors to the balcony and the cat tore out and around the corner.

Not hungry enough for a meal, Julie sliced an apple and some cheddar cheese, poured herself a glass of chardonnay and joined Sol – who was now sprawled across her outdoor table watching the squirrels – out on the balcony.

Ensconced in her lounge chair with her little repast at her side, Julie considered her next move. She would see Evelyn Hoag tomorrow. She sipped her chardonnay thoughtfully, reflecting on the fear she had felt earlier, accepting the fact that it would likely be with her until she caught him. But catch him, she would.

I was never afraid to go down *those stairs.*

56

Evelyn had already committed herself to help a friend move during the day, so Julie arranged to meet her at Hue, a Thornton Park restaurant, at six that evening. No day had ever gone so slowly. It was all she could do to return her calls and proofread her revision of *Clues*. Julie kept looking at her watch, willing the time to go by.

At five o'clock, she left the office and went home to let Sol out on the balcony. She thought about calling Joe to update him, but decided to wait until she had talked with Evelyn.

I need as much evidence as possible to convince him that Dianna had a stalker.

Unable to wait any longer, at five-thirty she got on her scooter and took off for Hue.

Julie was sitting at an outside table when Evelyn arrived at five past six. The shared interest in solving Dianna's murder had created a bond between them – much as it had with Julie and Kate Winslow – and they hugged awkwardly and took their seats.

Julie had been sitting there for a half-hour and the waiter appeared almost immediately upon Evelyn's arrival to take their order. After he left, Julie got right to the point.

"Do you remember Dianna ever speaking about a guy who was bugging her?"

"No. I don't remember her ever saying anything like that. Why?"

"I think she had a stalker who may have killed her."

"A stalker?"

"Yes," said Julie. "Two people have described the same man: Early thirties, tanned, a light natural blond with blue eyes, under six-feet tall."

"Good God. I think I've seen him, too!" said Evelyn.

"Where? When?"

"Just before she died," said Evelyn. "I met her for dinner near her place, at Seasons 52 on Sand Lake Road. We were sitting at the bar, waiting for a lakeside table out back. He waved and sent us drinks. She didn't say anything about him – we were talking about something, I don't remember what – she just sort of nodded 'thanks'. I assumed he was someone she did business with…another realtor or something.

"But then, when we went out to our table he came over. I could see he was taken by her, but that didn't strike me as odd. I mean...who *wasn't*? The only reason he stands out in my mind is that he was so *rude*. He pulled up a chair, turned his back to me and launched into a monologue. Dianna couldn't get a word in.

In fact, she apologized for him after he left."

"Did she insult him?"

"Hell, no. I thought she was unbelievably patient, considering what a bore he was."

"Can you remember what she said to him?"

"Something about it was 'nice', but he 'shouldn't have sent the drinks', she 'had a boyfriend'. She was obviously trying to get rid of him, but she was polite about it."

Dr. Jordan's words sprang into Julie's head:

"*...his victim may have been nice to him. But when he inevitably becomes intrusive, she puts her foot down. Suddenly, in* his *eyes,* he *becomes the victim.*"

"Did Dianna mention his name?"

"Let me think," said Evelyn. "He started in talking so quickly, I don't think she had time to introduce him." She looked down and to her left, her chin resting on her hand. She looked up, triumphant.

"His name was 'Hal'. She called him *Hal*."

———

Julie was so excited she couldn't get to sleep. She dialed Joe's cell phone.

"*Hi, this is Joe Garrett. I'm sorry; I'm not available right now. Leave your name and number and I'll get right back to you as soon as I can. Talk to you soon.*"

"Hi, it's Julie," she said, reminding herself to talk quickly before voicemail cut her off. "Don't get mad, but I've done some more investigating. Dianna had a stalker, Joe! I don't have his last name, but his first name is '*Hal*'. He's blond and blue eyed, Nordic or Scandinavian, under six-feet tall and tan…probably works outdoors. I know you'll be able to find him! He's been identified at her office, at the YMCA and he followed her to at least one restaurant. And she pissed him off, Joe! I'll tell you all about it when you get back…"

Julie hung up, feeling relieved. After a while, she even managed to fall asleep.

57

Even though the limit was only six lobsters per person per day in the Keys – as opposed to twelve in the rest of Florida – it was Joe's favorite place to dive. Nowhere else was the water as clear and the coral ridges - under which the giant crawfish hid - as breathtakingly beautiful.

Joe turned himself upside down in the deep aqua silence of the protected bay to search under a ledge of gently waving coral. A large grouper, undoubtedly after the same quarry, darted away at his intrusion. The bug was in there, face first, hiding among some sponges. Joe stuck his tickle-stick in behind the sponges and the lobster scrambled backward, right into his hooped net.

He's a big one!

Joe reminded himself that everything was magnified under the water. Still, there was no need to measure this one, he was certainly big enough to catch. He reached into the net to extract the trapped lobster and transfer him to his catch bag, which already held five others. Although he wore rubberized gloves, Joe was careful to grab the creature from behind. The Florida crawfish had no pincer claws like its Northern relative, but it was covered with sharp horns and spines that had pierced many an unwary diver's gloves. He dropped the wriggling lobster, tail first, into the bag, and drew the string tight.

That's it for me. My second day...my limit.

Joe gave a powerful kick with his fins and headed for the brilliant, sunlit surface.

———

It was amazing how a few beers and a belly-full of lobster – in Joe's case, just the lobster – could start everybody on the beach yawning. Will's other diver-friends, Dave Kirchner and Manny Sanchez and their wives, had just said "goodnight", raving about what a fabulous time they'd had. Each man had pulled up twelve lobsters of varying sizes over the special two day "sport" mini-season. Will's wife, Carolyn, and the other two women had prepared sumptuous side dishes to go with the lobster tails, which had been buttered, wrapped in tin foil and grilled. They had all agreed that it was their absolute, best *ever* cookout.

Carolyn was already in the front seat of Will's black Hummer as Joe and Will finished loading all the beach stuff into the back.

"What's the matter, old buddy? You looked bummed," said Will. "You have a good time?"

"Oh, yeah, I had a ball. Just missing Julie, I guess. I should've made her come down."

"Yes, you should have," said Will, wagging his finger at Joe. "Why don't you call her?"

"I can't. My phone's dead."

"Call her from the house."

"Nah, it's late. I'll call her in the morning…"

58

～

Julie was curled on her left side, facing the clock on her nightstand when she awoke. It was a quarter past six. She turned on the light and, out of habit, looked around for Sol. The big cat was still asleep, draped over the lower-right quarter of her queen-sized bed. Joe's old gray tee shirt was crumpled next to him.

Julie didn't remember stripping it off, but the room *was* warm.

She rolled onto her back, stretched and kicked the sheet down, waking Sol in the process. Slowly, she lifted her left leg straight up in the air and then lowered it, counting the repetitions. Then she repeated the exercise, flexing the leg as well. She finished the set - as her physical therapist had instructed – by making circles with her foot and ankle, first clockwise and then counter-clockwise.

Feels pretty good…

She got up, put on the tee shirt and padded, barefoot, over to the balcony doors. She opened them wide, stepping outside. Sol - not quite ready to start his day - stayed where he was on the bed, watching Julie with sleepy, half-closed eyes.

It was still dark and the early morning air coming across the lake was delightfully cool. Julie knew that wouldn't last long.

It's supposed to be in the middle nineties again today. Now is the time to go for a run, before the sun comes up. Wonder if I could?

She thought about it for a moment.

Sure, I could. Nice and easy...walk a little, run a little.

Smiling, Julie stepped back inside, locking the door behind her. Quickly, she pulled off Joe's tee shirt, swapping it for a tank top with a built in bra and a pair of shorts. She twisted up her hair and fastened it with a tortoise-shell clip that was lying in a box on her dresser; then she rummaged through a drawer, retrieving a low-cut pair of white cotton socks. Grabbing her sneakers, she headed out to the living room to put them on.

Julie no longer needed keys since Joe had put in the new lock, but she did take her little cell phone, tucking it into a zippered pocket on the left seam of the sport top. Although Sol had yet to make an appearance, Julie checked to make sure that his food and water dishes were full before she left.

She took the elevator, deciding to forgo the stairs.

That would be pushing it.

It was balmy and breezy outside. The sky was lightening some, the sun lurking below the horizon making the stars invisible. Julie stood for a moment enjoying the beautiful temperature, looking up at a fading half moon through swishing palm fronds.

There wasn't a car or a person in sight as Julie crossed Central Street to Lake Eola Park. She made her way down the familiar broad steps to the walkway that circled the lake and was soon striding along at a brisk pace, quite pleased with herself. She began to run, being careful to roll smoothly off her heel to her toe, minimizing the impact on her legs. It wasn't long, however, before she felt the strain and had to slow, once again, to a walk.

As she rounded the lake, Julie couldn't help thinking about Dianna Wieland. Once a lifeless stranger adrift on the lake, Julie now thought of Dianna as a friend. She had come to know her intimately...both the girl she had once been in Massachusetts...and the woman she had become in Florida. Dianna had been a complex human being, who had lived with regret and passion and hope.

She would have been a good mother.

Julie stood at the entrance to the boat dock, where the big swans, silvery in the pre-dawn moonlight, were all tethered and accounted for. A tear slid down her face as she bowed her head and remembered that morning:

Two Orlando Park Service employees were pedaling toward her on their city bicycles.

She waved both arms at them to stop.

"Hey!" she said, pointing at the fountain, "There's a woman in that loose swan boat!"

Their bikes had fallen to the ground as they hurried out on the dock.

"Christ, Hal. It is a woman!" the first one had said in shock.

Julie's head snapped up.

Hal.

The second guy's name was "Hal", and he never said a word. The other guy called it in. The other guy did all the talking to me and to the police, too.

Fiesta in the Park! The art show here at Lake Eola last November! Barry Costello said Dianna took a group of kids from the YMCA. That's when he first saw her. He probably got her name from one of the kids.

She would tell Joe as soon as he got back.

There was a noise behind her…

Suddenly every muscle in Julie's body was contracting in a total, mind-blowing charley horse. She collapsed immediately.

59

Bright daylight filtered through Carolyn Sawyer's ruffled, white guestroom curtains and on through Joe Garrett's eyelids. He blinked and held up his left arm, focusing on his watch.

Five minutes to seven. Shit.

His arm fell back on the somewhat short, but cushy, double bed. For all the femininity of the room, Joe had to admit it was comfortable; he'd slept like a played out puppy. The only problem was that he'd intended to be back in Orlando by nine. He'd forgotten to set the alarm on his watch.

He got up and went into the adjoining bathroom, remembering that he'd showered the night before, not wanting to get into Carolyn's pristine white sheets coated with salt water and sweat. He dug out his toothbrush from his leather shaving kit and began to brush his teeth vigorously while looking in the mirror. His skin was a couple shades darker and his hair was lighter from the weekend on the boat.

I need a haircut.

Maybe I'll let it grow. Merlin hates the buzz cut.

Thinking of Julie made him smile. He'd really missed her the last couple days.

Joe had already loaded his diving gear into the Land Rover. Now he straightened up the bed, threw his remaining stuff in his duffle bag and made his way out to the kitchen.

Carolyn was there, barefoot, in her shorts and tee shirt, drinking coffee and reading the paper. Joe guessed that she was probably in her late forties like Will. She was one of those lucky women like Julie, who looked good in the morning without makeup.

"Hey, there, good morning," she said. "Will said to say 'goodbye'; he had to get to the airport early. Want some coffee?"

Will, a helicopter pilot, was the owner of Sawyer Aerial Photography. Joe had met him years ago in the military and they'd been friends ever since. He recalled Will mentioning that he had a customer this morning, someone who was interested in the Everglades.

"Yeah, he told me last night. I was planning to get up early, too. That's one comfortable bed you've got there."

"I know. Isn't it great? It's got that thick pillow-top. Coffee?"

"You know, I need to get back to Orlando, Carolyn," said Joe, as he unplugged his phone from the charger on the kitchen counter. "I've got a travel mug out in the car, do you mind if I fill it?"

"Of course not. I'll slice you a piece of coffee cake to go with it."

———

Joe had finished his coffee cake and was cruising up the Florida Turnpike when he pulled his cell phone out of its holster on the dashboard and dialed up his voicemail.

"Received-July-twenty-fifth-at-ten-thirty-three-p-m," said the mechanical voice. "Press one to hear your messages now. Press two to…"

Joe pressed one.

"*Hi, it's Julie. Don't get mad, but I've done some more investigating. Dianna had a stalker, Joe! I don't have his last name, but his first name is 'Hal'. He's blond and blue-eyed, Nordic or Scandinavian, under six-feet tall and tan…probably works outdoors. I know you'll be able to find him! He's been identified at her office, at the YMCA and he followed her to at least one restaurant. And she pissed him off, Joe! I'll tell you…*"

The voicemail cut off the rest of her message.

"*That was your last message. Press one to hear your messages again. Press two…*"

Joe pressed one and listened to the message again.

Then he hung up and quickly dialed a number.

"*This is McPhee.*"

"McPhee. This is Joe Garrett. The guy that killed Dianna Wieland…it's Hal Johnson, the Parks Department security guy that was there that morning. Not Jesse what's-his-name…the other guy, the blond guy with the reflecting glasses."

"How do you know?"

"He was stalking her. Dianna Wieland took some kids from the Dr. Phillips YMCA to Lake Eola for an art show a few months before, then he showed up at the Y and her office and some other places. Merlin has people who can identify him," said Joe.

"Look, I'm on my way home from Miami, Patrick. I won't be there for two-and-a-half, three hours. I can't get a hold of Merlin and I'm really worried. I think that prick is the one who broke her leg. Will you check out her apartment for me? She's got keyless entry; I'll give you the code."

He hung up and speed-dialed Julie's cell phone again, but there was no answer.

Joe pulled into the passing lane, pedal to the metal.

60

The little phone was vibrating again in the zippered side-seam pocket of her tank top. The thought of the phone was Julie's only hope, even though she had no way to get to it. Hal had dragged her to his SUV and thrown her in the back. She was lying on her side, gagged and covered with a blanket. Her shoulders were pulled back painfully, and her wrists were tied to her ankles with what felt like a plastic tie. He had driven somewhere close to Lake Eola and parked and left her there. It seemed like hours went by as she lay there, trussed up and aching.

And then, suddenly, the car had started. They were on the move again. He was driving her somewhere… somewhere far this time.

Julie had never been so terrified in her life.

Hal Johnson drove slowly, passing only when he had to, being careful not to attract anyone's attention. Angrily, he thought of his tied-up passenger in back.

The bitch had finally figured it out. Hal had been afraid of this ever since he learned who Julie O'Hara was. He'd read about her in the newspaper. It was just his luck that the first person he saw after that fuck-up with Dianna was *Merlin*, a goddamn body language expert. He was so scared that morning! He'd been surprised she hadn't seen it. He felt in his gut that she would remember if she kept coming around the lake.

I should have killed her in the garage when I had the chance.

This was all her fault. He hadn't wanted to go this far, *but no*…she had to clamp onto this thing like a pit bull! Now he had no choice. Dumping her where no one would ever find her was the only way to deal with the situation. She had to disappear…and he needed an alibi.

After he tied her up, he'd gone home to his apartment in College Park, ten minutes from Lake Eola. The squat, U-shaped complex appeared to have been a motel at one time. It was a single floor, cement-block collection of twelve tiny apartments. Each one had a wall air conditioner positioned beneath jalousie windows, their front doors side-by-side. Hal left Julie in the SUV under a low-hanging tree, parked in the furthest space *behind* the building and entered through the rear door.

Once inside, he had called his boss at the Parks Department from his home phone and – coughing – said he was too sick to come into work. And then he waited. That was the hardest part, waiting almost two hours for his elderly, alcoholic neighbor, Tina Mae Cox, to wake up and turn on her TV. As soon as he heard it, he called her.

"Hi, Tina," he said, coughing loudly. "It's Hal. I hate to bother you, but do you have any Nyquil or cold medicine like that? I'm so sick, I haven't slept all night and I hate to drive 'cause I can hardly stand up."

"Oh, honey. You poor thing...sure I do. I'll bring it right over."

It only took a couple of minutes for her to go out her front door and knock on his. Hal called out from the bedroom for her to come in. That way, she could see that he was sick in bed and no one else was there. He thanked her profusely, and asked her to please close the blinds for him because he was going to try to sleep.

The moment Tina Mae left, he ducked out the back door, got in the car and took off.

61

~

Joe had received a call from Detective McPhee. He was at Johnson's apartment in College Park. Hal had played sick for his neighbor and his boss, but he wasn't at home and no one knew where he was. Confirming Joe's worst fear, Julie was nowhere to be found, either.

Joe arrived at her condo at half-past ten, keyed her code into the front door lock and headed straight for her computer. Sol rubbed back and forth across his legs as he sat at Julie's desk waiting impatiently for it to boot up.

All Joe's important information was stored on his Blackberry and he had a GPS application to track it in case the smartphone ever got lost. He had convinced Julie to do the same. If she had her phone – *and if it was on* – he could find her. When he got on the internet, he pulled up Julie's GPS app and entered her password, a play on words about her cat:

S o l a d u d e # 1
"Invalid Password"

S o l a d u d e 1
"Invalid Password"

Joe searched his memory. *"I thought I was your number one dude,"* he'd said.

He tried again, reversing it.

1 S o l a d u d e
"Please wait…"

Joe held his breath and waited.

And there it was, flashing on a map.

A map of the Ocala National Forest.

Oh, God. It's an hour away, and he's still moving!

And then Joe thought of someone who knew that area inside out. Someone who had loved Dianna Wieland. Someone Joe trusted, who could get to Julie fast.

62

Lincoln Tyler tore up the swerving, infrequently used trail at breakneck speed, whipping the big chestnut stallion over fallen trees and around palmettos. From Joe Garrett's description he knew *exactly* where Dianna's killer was taking Julie O'Hara. It scared him to think about it. Linc knew that time was of the essence without Joe's warning. The guy was headed down a long dirt road that dead-ended deep in the forest, about as far as a car could get coming from that direction. And there was nothing there... which pretty much told Linc what the bastard had in mind.

The trail soon intersected the narrow dirt road lined with pines. Linc pulled the blowing and dancing horse up short, leaning over, inspecting the ground. The afternoon rains had softened the hard clay and the fresh tire tracks were easy to see. Linc kicked the horse and took off down the road.

In moments he could see the SUV up ahead. The prick was standing in back of it, opening up the rear.

He heard Lincoln coming and slammed it shut.

"Uh…hi," he said, obviously astounded to find himself face-to-face with a man on horseback…and staring down the barrel of a gun.

Linc dismounted and looped the horse's reins on a branch by the side of the road.

"What are you doing out here?"

"Uh…uh…I was just taking a drive."

"Oh, yeah?" said Linc.

"I like to get out in the woods every once in awhile," said Hal, desperately.

Then Linc heard the muffled sounds coming from inside the SUV.

"I don't think so," he said, swinging the gun with all his might into the side of Hal's head.

Linc was shaking. He wanted nothing more than to shoot Dianna's bleeding, unconscious killer then and there. It took all his will to stick the gun back in his belt and pick up the keys lying next to the bastard.

But he swiftly grabbed them and opened up the back of the SUV. He pulled aside the blanket and there was Julie O'Hara, cruelly bound behind her back, wrist to ankle, like a hog-tied calf. Her eyes were wild with terror and pain. Quickly, he tore away the gag.

"AHH!" she cried, tears running down her face. "My hands! Get them loose!"

Linc pulled out his pocket knife and cut the nylon straps. Her wrists were raw and bloody.

He helped her straighten up and get out, crying and wincing, pain etched on her face. He took her in his arms.

"Shh. It's all right Julie. It's over…it's all right."

"J-Joe…where's Joe?" she asked, crying.

"He's coming. He'll be here. The police are coming, too."

The prick on the ground started to moan and move.

Linc looked at the oversized nylon ties he'd just cut off Julie's wrists and ankles.

"Hold this gun on him," Linc said, handing it to her. "Shoot him in the leg if he gets up."

Linc could see relief and anger replacing Julie's fear as she took the gun from his hand.

Quickly, he searched the car. He found a stun gun in the glove compartment. The cable tie gun was on the floor in back of the front seat. In short order, the two of them had the killer in the back of his own SUV, trussed up the same way he'd done to Julie. He was crying and his head was bleeding profusely. Linc didn't give a shit; he slammed the door on him.

"Where's your cell phone? That's how Joe tracked you."

Julie unzipped the side seam of her top, pulled out the phone and speed-dialed Joe.

"Joe? It's me…"

Lincoln could hear Joe's reply from a foot away.

"Julie! Oh, baby, I'm so glad to hear your voice!"

Clearly not as glad as she was to hear his…

Linc's horse, Applejack, was tethered too tightly to the tree on the side of the dirt road. Jack was pawing the ground anxiously and Lincoln stepped away to untie him and give Julie some privacy at the same time.

When she finished, he walked over to her, the horse trailing behind.

"I can't stay…you know that, Julie. You'll be all right now, won't you?"

She grabbed him and hugged him tight.

"Oh, God, yes! I'll be fine, Linc. *Go! Thank you.* I'll *never* forget what you did."

Lincoln swung up into the saddle and took off without looking back. The tension he'd been feeling melted away as he and Jack hooked a right onto the narrow horse trail and cantered off, deep into the woods where cars could not follow.

He felt good. There was no longer any bitterness, anger or frustration.

Linc saw Dianna's face…and she was smiling.

63

Evelyn Hoag was almost finished getting ready for work. She was in her large, carpeted bathroom, which doubled as a dressing room. Because she lived alone, most mornings she turned on the television - either in her adjoining bedroom or in the kitchen – for the illusion of company. The mention of Julie O'Hara's name caught her attention. She walked into her bedroom, the mascara wand in her hand.

The reporter was standing on a dirt road surrounded by trees and scrub brush.

"The body language expert, well known by Central Florida law enforcement as 'Merlin', had a harrowing experience yesterday, John. She was kidnapped, bound hand and foot, and taken here to the Ocala National Forest by an Orlando Park Service employee, Hal Johnson, a man who, according to the Marion County Sheriff's office, is a suspect in the death of Dianna

Wieland. You may remember, John, that she was the real estate agent from southwest Orlando whose body was discovered in a Lake Eola swan boat last January. My sources in the Orlando Police Department tell me that there was a small blood sample, previously undisclosed and different from the victim's, taken from that paddle boat. So, perhaps there will be some resolution in that particular case stemming from this arrest. Back to you, John..."

Evelyn sat on the bottom of her bed, the forgotten mascara wand resting in her lap, rivulets of dark tears staining her cheeks.

64

The Ocala Observer was the only newspaper that focused on the "mysterious cowboy" angle of the thwarted abduction in the Ocala National Forest:

LONE RANGER RIDES AGAIN
By Frank Maxwell

Was it one of Ocala's own? Most of the local residents think the mysterious cowboy-hero that saved a kidnapped Orlando woman in the 382,000 acre Ocala National Forest last week came from one of our local horse farms. There is no doubt, according to the Marion County Sheriff's department that, had the man not happened along at that exact moment, Julie O'Hara might well have been killed.

The victim, a respected body language expert, has described the horseman as "tall and dark, possibly Hispanic". The sheriff's office was unable to get a clear description from Hal Johnson, the alleged kidnapper, who said the man "was riding a huge horse and had a gun".

Apparently, the mysterious cowboy pistol-whipped the alleged abductor.

The article went on to quote several people from some of the twelve hundred horse farms in the area, none of whom had an inkling of who the man was, although it was widely speculated that he might be an illegal immigrant.

EPILOGUE

They were a family of four visiting Orlando for the first time, two teenage daughters with their mom and dad. Laughing, they helped each other climb out of the Lake Eola swan boats in the warm midday sun.

Julie, in a white halter top and khaki shorts, sipped her iced tea and watched them from the patio of the lakeside restaurant. Joe sat across from her, looking comfortable in a faded blue tee shirt and jeans.

Eleven months had passed since the arrest of Hal Johnson.

"What are you thinking about?" asked Joe.

"Dianna. It seems surreal that she could have fled here…died here."

"I'm sure she's at peace now, Merlin."

"Yes. I feel that she is."

Julie went back to her lunch, musing.

In retrospect, it was easy to see why the crime scene investigators thought Dianna had been alone on the boat dock. All the footprints in her blood had been accounted for, including those of the two Park Service employees who had come upon the scene at the start of their shift... and "blundered" onto the dock, to quote the defense.

Hal Johnson's single drop of blood on the neck of the swan - which had been drifting out in the middle of the lake - turned out to be the one piece of evidence his attorney couldn't overcome.

The Silver Swan,
when death approached,
unlocked her silent throat...

"You know, Joe, I believe we're all connected in a cosmic way that transcends time. Think about it... that fortune teller who nearly predicted Dianna's flight to the swan boat... and the madrigal, written so long ago, calling out to Dr. Jordan."

Joe leaned across the table. "Funny you should mention that," he said, lifting a lock of coppery-brown hair, his hand lingering on her bare shoulder. "I was just thinking about being connected..."

"Ah," said Julie, smiling. "An afternoon delight?"

Joe stood up, holding out his hand.

"I promise to make it cosmic..."

TURN THE PAGE
FOR A PREVIEW OF

MYSTRAL
MURDER

JULIE O'HARA
MYSTERY SERIES,
BOOK THREE

>>>

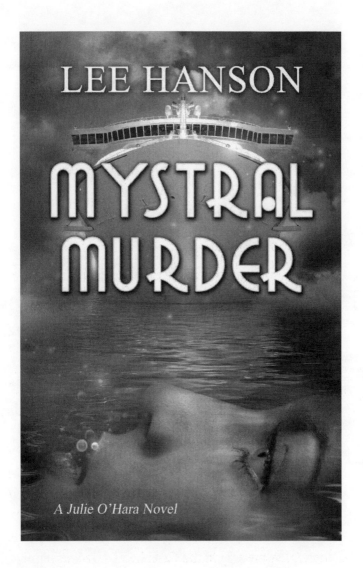

LEE HANSON

MYSTRAL MURDER

A Julie O'Hara Novel

MONDAY

1

The questioner stood, a broad-brimmed straw hat casting a shadow across her face. She was very thin and tan, a stylish woman in her forties wearing a slim, white linen sun-dress, perfect for a cruise. "Julie, as a body language expert, do you sometimes find out things you really don't want to know? Like secrets about friends or relatives?"

Everyone in the packed seminar looked expectantly at Julie O'Hara, who was seated on a stool in front of a large screen depicting a series of classic facial expressions. She glanced at her boyfriend, Joe Garrett, a private detective, who was accompanying her on this business/pleasure trip to the Caribbean. He was sipping on a Coke at a table a few rows back in the large

Odyssey cocktail lounge, a venue Julie had chosen over the ship's gigantic theatre. A smile played over his face as he watched her squirm, knowing that she wished he wasn't there.

"That's a very interesting question. Unfortunately the answer is yes. But, fortunately, most of them aren't holding out on me."

A ripple of laughter ran through her audience, including Joe.

"Seriously, though, most of you are probably quite good at spotting deception in people you know. Let's say a man is lying to his wife about something. Very often he'll give himself away verbally. It's hard to miss it when he hesitates before he answers the question, "Where were you last night?"

More laughter…

"And then, of course, when he starts giving you a whole lot of irrelevant information, he's a dead duck."

Every woman in the room was laughing out loud now.

"Okay, so a savvy philanderer might know better than to do any of those things," Julie said, laughing. "But he'd still have a hard time fooling his wife. On a subconscious level, we're all wired to notice signals in each other's body language. Especially faces," she said, indicating the screen behind her.

She rose and walked a couple steps closer to her audience, her hands open.

"Truly, it's a skill anyone can improve if they know what to look for. In the case of our hypothetical straying husband, his wife might pay particular attention to his *eyes*. A liar tends to blink more often and his pupils may be dilated, too. And those are just a few of the 'tells' our men can't control, Ladies. I hope you'll buy my book and learn the rest. We need to stay one step ahead of these guys."

Everyone was laughing again; it was a good time to wind things up.

"I had a great time today. I hope you did, too. Thanks for coming!"

Julie made her way through the applause to the book-signing table set up just outside of the lounge, stopping to shake a hand here and there. One old gentleman took her hand in both of his and said, "Did anyone ever tell you that you look like Julia Roberts?" The man's wife shot him a look you didn't need to be an expert to interpret.

"Yes, thank you," she said for the umpteenth time. She smiled at both of them and quickly moved along out of the lounge. Joe was already out there unpacking some additional books. He smiled at her and winked his approval.

I may not be Julia Roberts, but I'm a hell of an actress. Who ever thought I'd be doing this?

Writing *Clues, A Body Language Guide* had seemed like a logical next-step in her career, but Julie had never thought past the writing part, never thought of all the publicity and marketing involved in publishing. She had underestimated both the demands on her time and the loss of privacy.

Did I want the book to be a success? Yes, of course.

Did I want a guest spot on The View? NO.

She and Joe were aboard Holiday Cruise Lines' Mystral on a seven-day trip to St. Thomas, St. Maarten and back again, courtesy of her publisher. They had departed three days ago from Port Canaveral in Central Florida, just an hour from Orlando where the two of them lived and worked. The experience *was* exciting, she had to admit.

At the dock, the immense white ship had looked like a sixteen-story building several blocks long, truly an awesome sight. Since both of them were first-time cruisers, there was no denying the thrill they'd felt upon boarding. They had joked about being short-changed on what HCL considered 'Day 1', since the Mystral had set sail at exactly four-thirty in the afternoon on Saturday, when most of the day was gone. They would return to the same port the following Saturday, at six in the morning.

Yesterday, Sunday, the ship had stopped at Parrot Cay, a small island owned by HCL. It was a pure vacation day for Julie and Joe, who had gone ashore, enjoyed the ship's Caribbean Barbeque and spent the afternoon sunning and swimming.

But now, on Day 3, Julie felt like her vacation was over. She had just completed the *Clues* seminar, which was her first scheduled event. Later in the week, she had an open interview with Conde Nast Traveler magazine. Book signings were *de rigueur*, and Julie had to step out of her comfort zone each time to deal with her new, larger audience.

Corporate consultant, trainer, author…none of those hats seemed to fit well.

In the last few years, Julie's focus had changed dramatically. Using her skills in a more meaningful way had become paramount. For example, if not for this cruise, she'd be in Orlando helping select a jury. The defendant had shot a stranger coming through her window in the dark…a stranger who turned out to be her abusive ex-boyfriend. In Julie's opinion, the woman's body language confirmed that she was telling the truth, that she had no idea it was him when she pulled the trigger.

The guy's family, a rough bunch, didn't agree and were calling it murder.

Long story short, Joe was happy to have her safely signing books.

Julie sighed in frustration.

What's so safe about a floating skyscraper?

2

Cathy Byrne stepped into the Penthouse Suite and took off her broad-brimmed straw hat, setting it on the top shelf of an entry-way closet full of empty luggage. She could see that her husband, Gill, was on his way out. He was dressed for the warm summer weather in khaki shorts, a golf shirt and topsiders. *No doubt hoping to leave before I got back*, she thought.

What was it about men that they looked better as they got older? Of course, at six-four and broad-shouldered, Gill had always looked good. But now, at fifty-five with that thick silver hair and a perpetual tan, he was striking. He never gained weight, never had to diet. Lines only gave his face more character. *It's not fair*, Cathy thought.

"Where are you headed?"

"Oh, out and about," Gill said. "Captain Collier invited me up to the bridge. How was the seminar?"

"It was very interesting. You should've gone."

"Last night wiped me out; I never expected that game to go so long. I just got up an hour ago," he said, rummaging around on the granite bar looking for his card key.

"It's on the coffee table."

"Oh, thanks," he said grabbing it, heading for the door. He stopped and gave her a peck on the cheek. "See you later. I'll be back in time to get dressed for the Captain's Table."

Just like him to forget about me and do whatever he feels like.

Gill Byrne was a charmer who was used to doing whatever he wanted to do, whenever he wanted to do it. Five years ago, he sold his highly successful national beer distributorship to a global beverage wholesaler for millions. A smart investor, he had doubled his net worth since then and was currently buying every available building in Downtown Orlando.

Gill had acquired wives along with wealth. He married the first one at the tender age of twenty-five; she was only eighteen. Childless, they parted company five years later. The second time around was a shotgun wedding that ended when his daughter, Deidre, was eight. Gill never missed wife number two, but he'd spent the last several years trying to buy his daughter's affection. Not so much because he loved her, but mostly because he had a compulsion to charm everybody. As a result, Dede Byrne was spoiled rotten.

Cathy Byrne was wife number three.

At forty-eight, she took pride in looking several years younger. Turning, she caught her slim image in the mirror on the door. She turned sideways to look even slimmer. The white linen dress looked good with her tan, she thought, sucking in her stomach. *I could stand to lose a few more pounds, though.* She smiled and turned away, looking out the open glass door to the sea.

The large Penthouse Suite where she and Gill were staying was on Deck 10. It was tastefully decorated in soft gray and pale blue, and had a wall of glass with triple sliding-glass doors. The view was simply unparalleled. Adrienne Paradis, Cathy's friend and travel agent, knew that they wouldn't settle for less. And why should they? This was their fifteenth cruise with Holiday Cruise Lines; they were members of the privileged Captain's Club.

Cathy grabbed a Diet Coke out of the refrigerator under the bar and headed for the double balcony. She stood out at the railing, enjoying the warm breeze and the salty air. She really didn't have a care in the world. Except for one thing…

Cathy Byrne was wife number three.

Lee Hanson, a Boston native and Florida transplant, is the author of The Julie O'Hara Mystery Series, including *Castle Cay, Swan Song* and *Mystral Murder*. Her novels, featuring body language expert, Julie O'Hara, have been called "the answer to a mystery addict's prayer", a line that makes the author smile…and keeps her writing.